CEDAR'S BOY

by the same author

THE BLACK BUCCANEER

LONGSHANKS

RED HORSE HILL

AWAY TO SEA

LUMBERJACK

WHO RIDES IN THE DARK?

T-MODEL TOMMY

BOY WITH A PACK

CLEAR FOR ACTION!

BLUEBERRY MOUNTAIN

SHADOW IN THE PINES

THE SEA SNAKE

THE LONG TRAINS ROLL

JONATHAN GOES WEST

BEHIND THE RANGES

RIVER OF THE WOLVES

CEDAR'S BOY

WHALER 'ROUND THE HORN

BULLDOZER

THE FISH HAWK'S NEST

SPARKPLUG OF THE HORNETS

THE BUCKBOARD STRANGER

GUNS FOR THE SARATOGA

SABRE PILOT

EVERGLADES ADVENTURE

THE COMMODORE'S CUP

THE VOYAGE OF THE JAVELIN

WILD PONY ISLAND

BUFFALO AND BEAVER

SNOW ON BLUEBERRY MOUNTAIN

PHANTOM OF THE BLOCKADE

THE MUDDY ROAD TO GLORY

STRANGER ON BIG HICKORY

A BLOW FOR LIBERTY

TOPSAIL ISLAND TREASURE

STEPHEN W. MEADER

CEDAR'S BOY

ILLUSTRATED BY LEE TOWNSEND

HARCOURT, BRACE & WORLD, INC.
NEW YORK

CEDAR'S BOY

ONE

A BEAM of early morning sun, bright with September gold, came in the east window of the little bedroom and caught Shad Davis squarely on the bridge of his nose. He frowned in his sleep and moved his head but there was no escaping from the shaft of sunlight.

After a few seconds of struggle he opened his eyes and threw off the sheet that had covered him. Daylight, he thought. Time to get up—get the chores done—start for school. Then a happy thought crossed his wakening senses. This was Saturday! And more than that, it was the Saturday before the opening of Riverdale Fair! A whole wonderful week of no school stretched ahead of him—the most exciting week of the year!

Shad bounded out of bed. He was whistling *Camptown Races* as he pulled a shirt on over his head and buckled the belt of his jeans around his slim midriff.

He had earned his nickname by being the skinniest kid in school when he was ten. Now, at sixteen, he had added some muscle to his frame but he was still long and lean in build.

For a moment he stood at the window, looking across the field toward the river and the old woolen mill. It was going to be a hot day. Even now, in the dewy morning, a katydid was shrilling somewhere close by.

From below in the kitchen, his parents' voices came up to him clearly.

"That's all right," his father chuckled. "Fair Week only comes once a year. Let him go, soon as he's done your errands."

Then the screen door slammed and he heard the grind of the starter as the car engine chugged into action. Myron Davis was off to his day's work as superintendent of the brickyard.

Shad washed and went down to breakfast. A steaming bowl of oatmeal and a pitcher of milk awaited him on the kitchen table, and a pan of blueberry muffins sat on the back of the stove.

"Is that you, Melvin?" his mother called from the next room. "Dad says you can go to Riverdale if you like, but you're to get all your chores done first. There are some things I want at the store, too."

"Okay, Ma," he answered, and plunged his spoon into the oatmeal.

Breakfast eaten, he raced through his tasks. He split an armful of kindling, filled the woodbox with chunks of birch and maple, and picked a basket of Grimes Goldens from the big apple tree in the back yard.

"What do you want me to buy, Ma?" he called, as he wheeled his bicycle out of the shed.

His mother came to the back door. She was a small, spare woman, erect and quick-motioned. Whether she was making a bed, sweeping a floor or rolling out pie-crust, she moved with the determined swiftness of a swooping hawk. When she smiled her stern face became almost beautiful.

At this moment, however, she was preoccupied. A little frown wrinkled her smooth forehead.

"I wish I had some Rhode Island Greenings," she said, half to herself. "Those Grimes apples are fine for eating but they're not tart enough for a good pie."

"Gee, Ma—you going to take an apple pie to the Fair?" Shad asked eagerly.

"I don't know yet. I might if I could find the right apples. Maybe I can get some from Aunt Martha."

"You sure ought to," said the boy. "You make the best pies in the world. You'd win in a walk."

"Well, we'll see," she answered with the flash of a smile. "One thing I've put on this list is old-fashioned brown sugar. Without that a pie's pretty flat-tasting."

She handed him a scrap of paper with a dozen items

scribbled on it, and carefully folded a five dollar bill which she placed in his shirt pocket.

"Be sure you don't lose the money or the change," she warned. "It's all I've got to last till pay day."

Shad jumped on his bike and whirled out to the street, pedaling fast across the bridge. In the mill the looms were beginning to clack. On the end of the brick building a black sign with faded gilt letters bore the name "Squantic Woolen Company." It was the principal industry of the village, and for more than a hundred years it had been turning out fine flannels and broadcloths.

As he passed the gate a monstrous roan mare came plodding out. Shad stopped, resting on one foot, marveling for the hundredth time at the size of the beast. She was pulling a low-wheeled dray, loaded with cases of finished cloth, bound for the freight station.

"Hi, Johnny," the boy called to the stout little

Frenchman who held the reins. "How much you hauling in that load?"

"Ho!" laughed Johnny Couture. "She's small one
dees tam'. Only 'bout two ton. Ol' Babe, she's tak' it
easy today."

He shook the reins over the mare's broad, speckled
back and she pulled the heavy dray up the rise as easily
as if it had been a grocery wagon.

The whole town was proud of Big Babe. She was a
sort of freak, part Belgian, part Canada chunk, but
bigger than the horses of either breed. Shad knew her
story by heart. The owners of the Squantic mill, old-
fashioned in their ideas, still refused to use trucks for
their hauling. For years they had clung to horse-drawn
drays, and their matched teams of drafters were famous
around the countryside.

Two years before, the French Canadian head teamster had gone up to Quebec to buy a pair of horses.
When he returned he had only one horse, but his
eyes were glowing.

"I fin' dees mare on leetle farm near T'ree Rivers,"
he said. "She's only two year old, but so beeg no odder
hoss can pull wid her. I try her out. Four—five—seex
beeg rock I put on stoneboat. She pull 'em lak' nothin'
dere at all. So I say, 'Dees filly, she's good as team—
she's Canada one!' An' I breeng her home."

Now four years old, the mare stood eighteen-and-a-
half hands high and weighed close to three thousand

pounds. She ate as much as two ordinary horses, but she did as much work as any pair in the stable.

At the village store Shad found two of his friends on similar errands. 'Poleon Doucette and Hank Wetherbee were both in his class at Riverdale High, and the three of them had been pals for years. Hank, big and strongly built, was a second-string tackle on the football squad. 'Poleon preferred baseball. He was fast, compact, and his batting eye and ability to handle hot grounders made him a star shortstop.

"Hi, Shad," the French lad greeted him. "Goin' up to the Fair Grounds with us?"

"Try and stop me," Shad grinned. "How soon can you get off?"

"We'll both be ready as quick as we've got the groceries home," said Hank. "Meet us up at the swimmin' hole at nine."

As Shad climbed on his bicycle, balancing the heavy bag of food, he saw a shiny red truck rolling past the store. Through its small windows he caught a glimpse of tossing heads and alert ears. It was a horse van, carrying trotters to the Fair.

A grin of delight spread across the boy's face. Almost since he could walk he had had a passion for horses, and the part of Fair Week that always thrilled him most was the harness racing.

He deposited his groceries in the kitchen, left the change on the table and put his bike away in the shed.

The Fair Grounds were only two miles from Squantic Village by the highway, but for a reason of their own the boys had chosen to go up the river—a twisting route of four or five miles.

Shad reached the swimming hole a minute or two before the others. It was a pleasant spot on the river bank, shaded by overhanging trees. The bare feet of generations of Squantic boys had stripped the bank of grass, but there was deep, clear water and a sandy bottom.

Out of habit Shad began taking off his clothes as he approached the bank. He had thrown his shirt across a tree limb before he remembered, and he was hastily buttoning the last button when Hank and 'Poleon came racing down the path.

"Boat still there?" 'Poleon panted.

"I didn't look yet," said Shad. "Just got here myself."

The boat was a battered old flat-bottomed skiff that had floated down to Squantic one spring on the high water. The boys had fished it out, patched the holes and whittled out a makeshift pair of oars. It was hidden in a thick clump of alders, fifty yards upstream.

"She's here all right," Hank reported, as he pushed the leaves apart. "An' so's the tin can. Guess we'll need that. She's been out o' water so long we'll have to bail her plenty."

They got the clumsy craft into the river and Hank

started rowing. As fast as water poured in through the leaky seams, Shad and 'Poleon took turns bailing it out. Until the bottom boards began to swell they were too busy to pay much attention to the scenery.

Where the Caterwaul River came down from the hills it was a brawling, fast-running stream, full of falls and rapids. Here, between Riverdale and Squantic, it flowed along placidly, taking its winding course through pine woods and farmlands.

At the end of half an hour the skiff rounded a point and skirted a high bluff. Just ahead the boys saw a rickety landing of planks, on which an elderly man was sitting, smoking a short clay pipe.

He was a queer-looking figure, gray-haired and very fat. His only garment was a pair of tattered overalls, and he sat with his bare feet trailing in the water. Behind him the steep bluff was terraced into paths, between which grew rank on rank of huge dahlias. They made a mass of gorgeous color reaching all the way to the trees that lined the top of the bank, fifty feet above. A small, neatly painted shack perched on the crest in the shade of the pines.

"Mornin', boys," the old fellow called cheerily. "Bet I know where you're headed."

"Morning, Joe," they answered in chorus.

"Come on ashore, if you ain't in too big a hurry to git to the Fair Grounds," the fat man chuckled. "Like to show you my flowers."

Hank swung the bow of the skiff toward the bank and they tied up to the landing with a frayed piece of rope.

Their host jumped up with remarkable agility for a man of his years and poundage. He slid his bare feet into a pair of floppy carpet slippers and led the way up the bluff.

"Gosh, Joe," Shad exclaimed. "You've sure got a heap of dahlias. All different, too, aren't they?"

"Yep. I've got twelve hundred varieties this year. That ain't many, though. There's more'n twenty thousand kinds in all, so mine are only a drop in the bucket. Been crossbreedin' to get a couple o' new ones myself. They're up on Avenue A—that's the path nearest the top o' the bank. Here—look at this one."

He stopped beside a huge plant as high as his head, and pointed to a rich yellow bloom that was nearly the size of a dinner plate.

"That's a Royal Sultana," he said. "The big black one yonder's a King Kong. Over here's a Santa Claus. Red and white. Ain't it a beauty?"

The boys stared at the immense blossoms openmouthed. Each of the hundreds of plants was beautifully watered and tended. Along the narrow terraces the old man had dug trenches filled with black earth and compost that gave his flowers size and strength. And the slope, facing south to catch the sun, did the rest.

They reached "Avenue A" at last. Out of breath but beaming, old Joe turned to face the boys proudly. "I've been tryin' for eight years to get this one just right," he said. "Might call it my life work. But she's all set now. I call her 'Caterwaul Queen'—after the river, here."

He swung around dramatically and gestured toward a magnificent bloom. It was a full eight inches across and a rich maroon in color. Only the outer ring of petals was tipped with gold.

"Gee!" breathed 'Poleon. "She's a sweetheart for sure! What'll you do with a flower like that, Joe?"

The old fellow smiled. "Don't tell nobody," he said in a low voice, "but I aim to put her in the horticultural exhibit at the Fair!"

Properly impressed, the boys promised to keep the secret, thanked the old gardener and went back to their boat.

"He's a queer old duck," said Hank, when they were out of earshot. "Wonder where he came from. He sure can raise dahlias."

"My Pop told me about him," Shad replied. "Said he used to be a circus clown. His right name is Joe Banty. The show he was with went broke an' he came up here an' bought that little piece of river bank for twenty dollars. He's been growing flowers on it ever since."

"What's he do—live there all alone?" asked 'Poleon.

"I guess so. He used to have a half-wit son named Sam, but nobody's seen him around for years. Maybe the old man put him in an institution."

"Look, you guys—keep bailing," Hank warned.

Shad realized that water was sloshing around his feet and hastily set to work with the can. Soon the river made another bend. They could see scattered houses and the tall smokestack of a box factory in the distance. Nearer, along the top of the bluff on their left, was a weatherbeaten board fence, ten feet high.

"That's it!" cried 'Poleon. "Good ol' Fair Grounds!"

"Don't holler so loud," Hank growled. "Somebody up there'll hear you an' next week we'll have to pay our way in. How am I headin', Shad? D'you remember the place?"

"Sure—keep on about a hundred feet. It's right by that big willow."

They worked the skiff in close to the bank and Shad grabbed a low-hanging branch. In another moment the old boat was completely hidden under the willow boughs. The boys made her fast to a stump and got out, moving as quietly as possible.

The steep bank above them was covered with a mass of wild grapevines and creepers. Shad took the lead. He climbed cautiously, hunting for safe footholds, testing his weight on the vines. When he reached the top the others were right behind him.

"Okay?" he whispered. "Here's the loose board. I'll

take a look first an' see if the coast's clear."

Crouching, he put one eye to a crack in the fence. All he could see was a high growth of weeds and the rear of a low, frame building twenty feet away. He took careful hold of the bottom of the board and pulled it toward him. There was a creak of rusty nails but the board moved easily. In a matter of seconds Shad was wriggling through the foot-wide hole.

He waited in the weeds till the others had followed him. They could hear the champ of horses, eating their morning feed, but there were no men in sight.

Shad straightened up and grinned. "Well, we're in," he said. "Anybody coming with me to the stables?"

"Not me," answered Hank. "I'm headin' for the poultry house. Want to get a look at those big New Hampshire Reds. How about you, 'Poleon?"

"Chickens?" said the French boy scornfully. "Me— I'm goin' to watch 'em set up the Ferris wheel. Did you bring some money for lunch?"

Hank had change in his pocket but Shad had forgotten to bring any.

"Never mind," he told them. "Maybe I can pick up a quarter working around the stables. Meet you over by the grandstand at noon."

TWO

HE came around the corner of the old stable building and stood still for a minute, drinking in the remembered sights and sounds and smells.

A golden haze of dust rose across the sunlit acres of the Fair Grounds. Everywhere was busy preparation. Men shouted in the distance as they erected tents along the Midway. Trucks and cars chugged past over the uneven ground. Brush scrapers, pulled by small tractors, were at work on the half-mile oval of the track. And somewhere nearby a colored stable boy was humming *Joshua Fit de Battle of Jericho* as he curried a trotter. The pleasant, acrid odor of ammonia and horse sweat was all about him.

Shad hurried on till he came to the front of the long row of stables. Through the windows, screened to keep out the flies, he could see sleek heads—black and bay, brown and chestnut. He moved slowly along the line, pausing now and then to read the names of horses and

owners. They had come from all over New England
and beyond. There were trotters with the famous Hanover blood lines from Pennsylvania, and pacers whose
names told of descent from such great sires as Directum
I or Abbedale.

Riverdale Fair wasn't on the Grand Circuit, but its
purses were big enough to attract horses that were close
to big-time speed. Some of the names, in fact, Shad
recognized as Grand Circuit winners of the past season.

He was standing reverently before the stall of a handsome colt called Minstrel Direct when someone clapped
him on the shoulder.

"Shad Davis!" came a friendly chuckle. "I didn't
know you were a harness horse fan."

He turned to face a husky youngster of his own age.
It was Hartley Martin, Jr., generally known as "Bud."
His father was part owner of the big Mason & Martin
dairy farm up on Red Horse Hill. Bud was in Shad's
class at Riverdale High.

"Harness horse fan?" Shad grinned. "I sure am—
crazy about 'em. Your father owns some trotters,
doesn't he?"

"That's right. We've got three down here. Dad didn't
decide to race them till the last minute, so we drew the
worst stable of all—that old shack back by the fence.
If you're through admiring these fancy nags, come on
over with me and look at some real horses—New Hampshire bred."

They walked back through the dust toward the di-
lapidated building that stood close to Shad's private
entrance. From the front it looked more businesslike.
There were three box stalls at one end, a feed and
tack room, and an open shed under which the sulkies
stood.

"Ever hear of a horse called Cedar?" Bud asked.

Shad nodded. "Pop pointed him out to me once on
the street when I was a little kid," he replied. "He
was pretty old then, but handsome. Kind of a red sorrel color, wasn't he? I remember hearing how fast he
used to be on snow, too."

"That's right." Bud's face glowed. "I guess he was
the greatest snow-horse that ever raced around here.
My father drove him when he won the Riverdale Free-
for-All. That was thirty years ago, and Dad was just the
age I am now.

"After that, Uncle John Mason turned Cedar over to
Billy Randall, the trainer, and he raced on the Grand
Circuit for three or four years. He was a free-legged
pacer—one of the few that never had to wear hopples."

They were standing in front of the old stable now.
A white bull terrier with alert ears and a whiplike tail
came trotting out of the tack room. He looked up at
Shad, one eyebrow cocked questioningly.

"This is Tug," said Bud, stooping to scratch the
white dog's head. "Tug the Fourth. He travels with
the horses. They like him for company and he's a big

help keeping the rats out of the feed bins. Tug knows you're a friend of mine now, but if you were a stranger and came around here he'd never let you get within ten feet of the stable."

The door of the first stall opened and a small, dark man came out. His lively black eyes twinkled and he was whistling softly as he set down his bucket and currycomb.

"Hi, Yance," said Bud. "I want you to meet Shad Davis. He's in my class at school, and he's as much of a nut about horses as you are."

The man thrust out a wiry brown arm and shook Shad's hand.

"Good!" he answered with a grin. "Anybody that likes horses is okay with me."

"How's Cedar's Boy?" Bud asked. "Have you worked him yet?"

"No, I'll wait till the track's ready, this afternoon. He's feeling good, though. Ate a nice breakfast. Want to see him?"

He threw open the stall door and they drew closer to look at the big horse inside. Cedar's Boy was a bright bay in color, with red lights glowing in his glossy coat. He was tall and rangy but solidly put together. Powerful muscles rippled under his skin, his chest was deep, his legs clean and slim, and his polished hoofs generously proportioned. In the middle of his handsome forehead was a small, diamond-shaped star—the only white patch on his body. He had a fine head with calm, intelligent eyes and well-set ears, pricked forward in friendly fashion as he welcomed the visitors.

"Gosh," Shad breathed. "What a horse!"

Yance looked pleased. "That's right," he nodded. "He's the nearest thing to old Cedar we've ever had. Only a three-year-old, but he did a two-ten mile at Gorham last month. I don't know as he'll ever beat his granddad's time, but if he stays sound he ought to come close."

"What was Cedar's record?"

"One-fifty-nine-and-a-half," Bud replied. "But he paced in an even one-fifty-nine once on a straightaway mile over snow."

They moved on to the next stall, where a lean chestnut colt was nervously pawing and tossing his head.

"This is Redwood," Yance explained. "He's only a two-year-old and a bit edgy, but we think he's a likely youngster. After he steadies down he ought to have a lot of speed.

"And this little lady," he continued, pointing to the last box, "is named Sequoia. She's the only trotter in the Cedar line. Her dam was Sequel Hanover, so I guess her gait would naturally be a trot. But you can see Cedar blood in that red sorrel coat of hers. This is her third year of racing and she's good for two-twelve or two-fourteen any time it's needed."

Shad could hardly take his eyes off the lovely little

mare. When he turned to Yance at last, his face was eager.

"Do you s'pose I could work around here?" he asked. "I could carry water an' clean out the stalls, an' I'm a pretty good hand at grooming. I wouldn't want much pay—just lunch money is all."

Yance looked him up and down appraisingly.

"I could use some help, all right," he said. "We need somebody here while I'm working the horses. What do you think your Dad would say, Bud?"

"I think he'd like the idea," the boy grinned. "Anyhow, give Shad a tryout an' I'll speak to Dad about it tonight. Or better yet, why don't you come up to the farm tomorrow, Shad, and talk it over with him? We'll be home after church. Ride your bike up. There are some hills to climb, but the new county road's pretty good."

Shad agreed enthusiastically and Bud took his departure.

"I'm going over to the Livestock Building," he said. "Our truck'll be coming in pretty soon and I want to be there when they unload Mountain Majesty. That's our prize bull."

Yance led Shad into the tack room and took down a set of racing harness from its peg.

"Here's a job that needs doing right now," he said. "I'll show you how to clean it and oil it so the leather won't dry out and crack."

Shad learned quickly. In a few minutes he was seated on an upturned feedbox, working diligently at the supple leather straps while Tug watched him with approval.

By noon he had finished two sets of harness and Yance was obviously pleased.

"Good job," he said. "I reckon you didn't bring any money this morning, so here's some change to buy your lunch. I won't be needing you till three-thirty if you'd like to take a look around the Fair."

"Thanks—and I'll be back," Shad assured him. And with the half dollar Yance had given him he hurried off to meet his friends by the grandstand.

They were there, waiting. 'Poleon gave an exaggerated sniff and wrinkled his nose.

"Hoss!" he said wryly. "From the smell, I'd say you got a job at the stables, all right."

"Boy, you missed it!" Hank put in. "This is goin' to

be the best Fair ever. Y' oughta see the new side shows. An' those roosters over at the Poultry Building—big as turkeys!"

They walked back to the Midway and purchased hamburgers and ice cream cones. With lunch disposed of, the three boys set out to see the sights.

The Ferris wheel and the flying boats were already in place, and two big merry-go-rounds were being set up at one end of the amusement area. Sounds of hammering came from half-erected booths and tents and a steady procession of trucks rumbled through the dust, bringing new exhibits to the various buildings. Over in the parking area long rows of stakes were being driven to mark the lines for cars.

'Poleon steered them toward the Machinery Building. The great, barnlike structure was already well filled with marvels. There were brightly painted tractors, corn-pickers, potato-diggers, manure-spreaders and hay-loaders; power saws, lathes, drills and welding outfits; milking machines, pasteurizers and cream separators. In the household division they came to washing machines, vacuum cleaners, record players and radios.

"Hey—look!" cried 'Poleon. "Television sets! My ol' man saw 'em work when he went to Boston. He says they'll get a relay up here any time now, an' we can see big league ball games an' everything! Do you reckon they'll have one runnin' here?"

There was nobody present to answer the question, so they took samples of all the booklets offered and contented themselves with staring at the magic windows of the receivers, now blank and dark.

At Hank's insistence they visited the Poultry Building and were greeted by a tremendous crowing of prize cockerels and clucking of hens. Shad and 'Poleon had to admit that the big New Hampshires were handsome birds and would make mighty tasty roast chicken on the Sunday dinner table.

The Livestock Building was next door and they went in. Many of the stalls were still empty, for animals would be coming in as late as Monday morning. They passed pens of heavy-fleeced sheep and gigantic hogs and came at last to the dairy cattle section. Mountain Majesty stood in the middle of his oak-beamed stall. He was a magnificent buff and white Guernsey, with immense shoulders and a neck humped with muscle. The bull's head was lowered a little and he had a surly look in his eyes. Once he snorted and the ring in his nose jerked up and down.

"Gee," Hank murmured. "I bet if he wanted to he could bust out o' there in two shakes!"

"Yes, sir!" Shad put in proudly. "He's some bull, all right. He belongs to my new boss, Mr. Martin. You know—Bud Martin's father. I'm helping handle his string o' horses."

'Poleon laughed. "Helpin' handle 'em, huh? I suppose you'll be drivin' 'em in some o' the races!"

"Well, no," Shad admitted. "But maybe I'll get to exercise 'em. Say—I'm going to ride my bike up to Red Horse Hill tomorrow an' see Mr. Martin. How about coming with me?"

"What?" cried Hank. "**Ten miles, an' all upgrade? Not me!**"

"Nor me," 'Poleon chimed in. "There's a ball game tomorrow anyhow, an' I'm playin' short for the Squantic Woolens."

By three o'clock Shad was back at the stable. He ran out the exercise sulky and helped Yance put the harness on Cedar's Boy.

"You know," the trainer told him approvingly, "you've got a touch with horses. They like it when you lay a hand on 'em—don't seem to get fidgety. Maybe you've got gypsy blood in you, like me."

As the wiry little man gathered the reins and mounted the sulky seat, Shad looked at him and wondered. Gypsy blood. That would account for Yance's hawklike face and brown skin. He had never known a real gypsy but he had always heard they had a way with horses.

The big red pacer tossed his head and moved toward the track gate at a swinging, catlike walk. His bay coat glowed like fire in the afternoon sun. There were four or five other horses jogging around the half-mile oval. Yance guided Cedar's Boy out on the track, turned him to the right and gave him his head. The red horse was in no hurry. His stride lengthened gradually into the rocking gait of the true pacer and he went down the straightaway with his dark mane streaming in the wind.

Shad uttered a little sigh of pleasure. He had been standing there holding his breath in a sort of trance. "Gosh," he murmured. "Wouldn't I like to hold the reins over a horse like that!"

THREE

BREAKFAST on Sunday was always an event in the Davis household. There was no need for early rising, and Shad and his father lolled in their beds till eight o'clock or later. Then the pleasant fragrance of brewing coffee or the aroma of ham sizzling in the pan got them up in a hurry.

"You must have put in quite a day at the Fair Grounds," Shad's father remarked, as they sat down to their griddlecakes and maple syrup. "Your Ma says it was past dark when you finally got home."

"Yes, I guess it was kind o' late," the boy admitted. "What happened was, I got a job. The other boys weren't in any rush to start home, so I waited till the horses were bedded down. I'm a stable swipe now," he added proudly.

"Whose stable?" asked Mr. Davis.

"Hartley Martin's. You know him, don't you? The dairyman up on Red Horse Hill. He used to drive a pacer called Cedar."

His father nodded. "That's Bud Martin," he said. "Sure—I know him well. Mighty fine man. So he gave you a job?"

"Well—he didn't exactly. But young Bud an' the trainer both think it'll be all right, an' I'm going up to the farm today an' talk to Mr. Martin himself."

His father's eyes twinkled. "Quite a pull up those hills on a bike," he said. "I'll tell you what. Let's all take a ride in the car this afternoon an' drop in on 'em. What do you say, Mother? You haven't seen Polly Martin in a 'coon's age."

She looked doubtful. "You know I'd like to," she said. "But there's the brass and silver I ought to polish."

"No 'buts' about it," her husband told her firmly. "After a breakfast like this we don't need more'n a cold snack at noon. We can have it right after church an' get a good early start."

By one o'clock they were driving north out of River-dale with the hump of Blue Job Mountain looming ahead. Shad looked at the stiff grades up which the old Buick chugged and congratulated himself on the fact that he wasn't pedaling his bicycle through the noonday heat.

After a while his father pointed toward a shoulder of the mountain where the road went up in a white ribbon.

"That's the farm," he said. "See those long barns? It's a handsome place. They must have a hundred head o' Guernseys."

At the top of the hill they swung into a driveway between well-kept lawns. In the shade of a giant sugar maple tree stood a rambling white house, connected by a long shed with the nearest barn.

"Bud's added on to the old place," said Mr. Davis, "but he's kept it looking nice an' homelike. See that weathervane on the barn cupola? That's been a landmark up here since before I can remember."

Shad looked up at the spirited silhouette of a horse and a high-wheeled sulky, trotting bravely against the blue September sky. It made him feel good inside just to look at it.

Young Bud Martin was out on the porch almost before the car stopped.

"Hi, Shad!" he called. "Hello, folks. Come right in. Dad said he hoped you'd drive up."

Shad was introduced to Hartley Martin, Senior, and to his pretty, blonde wife, Polly. They all went through the living room and out to a screened side porch where a little old white-haired couple sat in rocking chairs.

"This is Aunt Sarah Mason," said Bud, "and Uncle John Mason. Here's a boy after your own heart, Uncle John. Shad's a real horseman."

The old man—he must have been over eighty—shook Shad's hand heartily. He was gnarled and bent like an old apple tree and his beard was snowy white, but his eyes still had a merry twinkle.

"Mighty glad to hear that," he chuckled. "Ain't enough folks in the world that really understand hosses. Kin you drive a trotter?"

"I'd like to try," Shad told him. "Yance says he'll let me exercise Cedar's Boy some time if I do my work right—and if Mr. Martin thinks it's okay."

He looked toward Bud's father questioningly, and Hartley Martin nodded.

"I take Yance's word on most things," he said. "It's all settled. You'll take your orders from him and get regular stable hand's wages for the work—thirty dollars."

He turned to Myron Davis with a grin. "There's just one thing," he added. "I know Shad won't mind, but you may. We'll want him to sleep at the stable. Yance is on the job most of the time, but he deserves an occasional night off."

Shad's mother frowned a trifle, but Myron Davis patted her arm. "It'll be fun for the boy," he reminded her. "Good as camping out. Sure—we'll agree to that, Bud."

The two youngsters left the older people chatting on the porch and went out to look the place over. They passed through the spick-and-span milk house, with its gleaming stainless steel equipment, and entered a big, airy barn, with long rows of stanchions running down either side of the floor.

"This is the milking barn," Bud explained. "We keep sixty cows in here. They're up in the pasture now, of course—all except this heifer in the corner stall. She was my 4-H Club calf last year and I won a blue ribbon with her. She'll have her own first calf in the next day or two. Isn't she a beauty?"

They went past two big silos and on into another barn. A handsome young bull stood in the first box stall behind stout oak bars. He chewed his cud placidly enough and eyed the visitors with mild interest.

"That's Passaconaway's Pride of Riverdale," said Bud. "I raised him, too, and Dad says he'll be every bit as good a sire as Mountain Majesty. He's a lot gentler, though. Majesty gets pretty ugly sometimes, and the men have a tough time handling him. This barn is where we keep the bulls and young stock."

"Where are the horses?" asked Shad, and his young host laughed.

"It's easy to see what you're really interested in," he said. "Well, we're coming to the horse barn next."

The building they entered was smaller than the others, but just as clean and well-kept. The half dozen roomy stalls were all empty.

"You already know the three that are down at the Fair Grounds," said Bud. "The others are out in the paddock. I'll introduce 'em to you."

Opening off the south end of the barn was a grassy

enclosure that covered an acre or more. A pretty bay
mare and her red-coated foal were browsing along the
white fence. And a little way off a slim chestnut filly—
a yearling, Shad thought—gave the newcomers a wide-
eyed look, then flirted her tail and raced off around
the paddock

"The old lady here is Cinderella Girl," said Bud.
"She's our brood mare—a daughter of Cedar. Used to
be pretty fast herself, ten years or so ago. The little
colt is Caribou II, named after Cedar's sire. And that
crazy young thing that was making eyes at you is Polly
Flinders. If she ever grows up and gets some sense,
she might have more speed than any of 'em."

Much as he admired Polly Flinders, Shad was drawn
irresistibly to the mare and her foal. The long-legged
little colt stood by his mother's side and regarded the
visitors with childlike interest. He was a bright bay
color all over except for a tiny white star in the middle

of his forehead. From his ridiculously round little rump a short, fuzzy tail whisked gaily up and down.

"Doggone!" murmured Shad. "He's the cutest little cuss I ever laid eyes on. Look at those legs, an' the proud way he holds his head. I bet he'll make a race horse!"

The colt tossed his woolly little mane and went rocking away to the other side of the enclosure.

"Hey, look—he's pacing!" Shad exclaimed. "He must be a natural pacer!"

"That's right," said Bud. "There are mighty few of 'em, but he's one—just like his granddad and his great-granddad. That's why we called him Caribou. Did you ever hear that caribou are the only kind of deer that don't trot or gallop? They're sure-enough pacers, and boy—can they travel!"

As they climbed upward toward the pasture, Bud told Shad the story of old Cedar's birth on the night of one of the wildest blizzards that ever swept the New Hampshire hills.

"Dad used to say that was what made him such a great snow-horse," the boy chuckled. "Anyhow, it's a fact that he always raced best in winter, when he was pulling a cutter on the snow-path."

They came to a clump of gnarled cedar trees, nestling in the shelter of the ridge. A plain granite slab beneath the trees bore the name *CEDAR* and two dates, twenty-five years apart.

"This is where he's buried," said Bud. "Right in the same spot where Dad and Uncle John found him with his mother, the morning after the big storm. Old-time horsemen come up here sometimes, just to stand and look. They all knew Cedar."

Shad had a reverent feeling as he stood before the grave marker. Neither of the boys had much to say as they started back toward the farm buildings.

After a while Bud broke the silence. "Cedar was stolen once," he said. "Did you ever hear about that? It's quite a story. I think he was only a two-year-old colt when it happened, and Dad was just a boy. Dad traced him all the way to Boston and finally got him back."

"Gosh!" said Shad. "Who was it stole him?"

"A gypsy horse-trader by the name of Harko Dan. He got a long stretch in state's prison for that and a couple of other jobs like it. Some day I'll get Dad to tell you the whole yarn. It was a pretty slick piece of detective work."

"I've heard folks say you couldn't trust gypsies," Shad said. "I sure like Yance, though, an' he's one, isn't he?"

"Yes, he's a gypsy, but he's one of the decent kind. Yance is as honest as anybody could be, and he's abso-lutely loyal to Dad and Uncle John. They took him in and were good to him when he was a kid. Just about saved his life, I guess. There's nobody better with horses than a square-shooting gypsy. Yance can practically talk to 'em in their own language!"

By the time they reached the house, Shad found his parents ready to start for home. He said good-by to the Martins and Masons.

"I'll be at the track good an' early tomorrow," he told Bud's father. "An' I'll be glad to stay there nights, too—as often as you want me."

"Good enough!" Hartley Martin grinned. "You'll see me down there myself, some time along in the forenoon."

When the Davis family got home Shad changed from his good clothes and rode his bike over to Hank Wetherbee's. It was close to suppertime and he found his friend out in the poultry yard feeding the chickens.

"What time can you get off tomorrow morning?" he asked.

"I dunno. Not before eight-thirty or nine anyway," Hank replied. "Too many chores to do first. Why—do you want to get up to the Fair Grounds early?"

"Yes, I promised Mr. Martin I'd be there and I don't want to disappoint him the first day. Guess I'd better ride up, then. You and 'Poleon can use the boat, and I'll be seeing you around the track. Stop at the stable on your way in. Maybe I'll have some time off later, and we'll take in the sights."

.   .   .

It was before sunrise when Shad tumbled out of bed on Monday morning. At seven he was pedaling his bicycle up to the main gate of the Fair Grounds. The crowds wouldn't start to arrive for another two hours, and he found only one sleepy ticket seller on duty.

"Hey," the fellow growled at Shad. "Fifty cents admission plus tax."

"I'm working here," answered the boy.

"Got a pass?"

"Not yet. I'm just starting this morning. Stable swipe for Mr. Hartley Martin."

The man hesitated. "If you're pullin' a flim-flam on me," he said, "you're goin' to get in trouble. I guess I'll let you go in this once, but don't try it again without a reg'lar pass."

Shad breathed easier as he rode through the gate. He had just twenty cents in his pocket.

The Midway, empty of people at this hour, shone in the morning sun, a-glitter with new paint and sleek white canvas. Every booth and side show tent was in place, ready for the opening-day throngs to arrive.

Riding down the broad thoroughfare, Shad could hardly take his eyes off the gaudy signs and banners along the way. Painted in vivid reds, blues, greens and yellows, they fairly screamed their messages.

The whole front of one tent was covered by a picture of "Little Fatima, Queen of the Harem, in her Daring Oriental Dances." She was shown as a scantily clad, curvaceous damsel with a veil coyly draped over the lower part of her face.

Next in line was a big booth where the proprietor was busily setting up his lures—fountain pens, canes, alarm clocks, pearl-handled revolvers and kewpie-dolls under a huge sign that read:

"Hoop-La! Circle the Prizes! 5 Hoops for 25¢!"

There were dozens of other attractions, including "Spun Sugar Candy—½ Bushel for a Dime!" . . . "Duke, the Dodger—Hit him on the Coco and Get a Cigar—3 throws for 5¢!" . . . "Ajax, the Biggest Ox in the World" . . . "Guess Your Weight for a Nickel —a Box of Candy if I Miss by more than 3 pounds!" . . . "KI-KO, the Wild Man—He Eats Raw Meat!" . . . and a new one Shad had never seen before— "NELLIE, the Only Real Mermaid in Captivity!"

The boy rested one foot on the ground while he stared at the colorful portrait of Nellie, the mermaid, reclining on a rock in the midst of blue waves and combing out her long, golden hair. Above the waist she was unmistakably a woman. Below, her body tapered to a single graceful tail, covered with fishy scales.

"Gosh!" Shad whispered to himself. "A real live mermaid! Prob'ly the only chance I'll ever have to see one. Wonder if she can talk, like human folks. I'll have to dig up a quarter an' see this one sure."

He left the Midway and rode past the Ferris wheel and the merry-go-rounds, motionless and silent now—

past the exhibit buildings, noisy with the lowing of cattle and the clarion calls of roosters—and on toward the great, roofed stands of the trotting track.

A dozen horses were taking their morning work-outs, and up and down the rows of stables there was a bustle of activity. He dismounted and leaned his bicycle against the end of the Martin stable. Tug trotted out to investigate, sniffed once at the legs of his dungarees and gave a short, satisfied bark to announce his arrival.

"That you, Shad?" called Yance. He came out of the feed room with a measure of oats in his hand and nodded a brisk greeting.

"Right on time," he said with a grin. "I had a hunch you'd be here early. Well, we've got plenty to do today. You can start by bringing a couple of pails of water from that spigot over by the big stable. After that we'll see what kind of a groom you are."

FOUR

WHILE Cedar's Boy and Sequoia were munching their breakfast, Shad helped the gypsy trainer harness the young pacer, Redwood. Attached to the horse's bridle and extending across the bridge of his nose was a big roll of sheep's wool.

"What's that thing for?" Shad asked.

Yance slipped the bit gently between the colt's velvet lips, tucked his ears in and buckled the throat-latch.

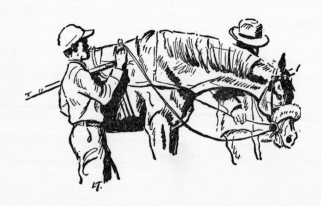

"That's a shadow roll," he explained. "Redwood's just a mite skittish, an' when he gets to pacing he's scared by the sight of his own forefeet reaching out there in front of him. Quite a few horses have that trouble. You'll see 'most as many with shadow rolls as without 'em."

The young horse fidgeted until he felt the sulky shafts buckled in place. Then he stood quiet, waiting for Yance to mount.

"I'll be out about an hour," the gypsy called over his shoulder as he gathered the reins. "You can go to work on the others. You'll find the brush and currycomb in the tack room."

Shad started with Cedar's Boy. He went into the box stall beside the big red horse and proceeded to get better acquainted. First he moved quietly up to the front of the stall, where Cedar's Boy could look him over and sniff at his hands. He talked to the big pacer in a low, friendly voice, stroking his neck and patting his shoulder. Then he produced the currycomb and began running it lightly over the satiny red coat. He started behind the ears and worked down over the strong neck and deep chest to the forelegs.

The horse stood calmly, enjoying every minute of it. Occasionally his supple skin twitched a little and Shad knew that meant the massage was pleasant to him.

"M-m-m," the boy murmured. "That's the spot.

Now we're getting the dust out. No more itches. Feels good, doesn't it?"

He went over every inch of him with the currycomb, then polished off the bay hide with the brush. When he got through, every glowing hair lay smoothly in place. In the tack room he found a bottle of oil and a rag which he used to shine up the horse's hoofs.

The job was just about done when Yance brought Redwood back from the track. The colt's chestnut sides were dark with sweat and there were white flecks of foam on his breast. Shad hurried out and held the bridle while the trainer climbed down.

"Looks as if you'd given him a real workout," the boy commented.

"Some o' that sweating's just nervousness," said Yance. "We just jogged most o' the time, but I breezed him the last half in ten."

"Ten?" asked Shad, a little confused. "Oh, I get it. A minute an' ten seconds—is that it?"

Yance grinned. "Right," he said. "You're catching on. How'd you make out with Cedar's Boy?"

He walked over to the stall and looked in. Then he whistled. "You got him shined up like a mahogany table," he said. "Good boy. Now we've got to get this youngster cooled out an' rubbed down."

They removed the harness from the colt, threw a light blanket over him and buckled a halter on his head.

"Walk him up an' down easy for about ten minutes," Yance told the boy. "You'll find him kind enough, now he's had his exercise."

Shad began the process of making friends with the colt while he led him slowly back and forth in front of the stable. Redwood was gentle as a lamb, now that he had worked off his surplus energy. By the time the cooling-out was over, he knew the young horse trusted and liked him.

Under Yance's supervision he rubbed down Redwood's sweaty flanks with a clean burlap bag. Finally, when the colt was thoroughly dry and had been watered and fed, he curried and brushed him till his hide shone like a new-minted penny. He was just putting the finishing touches on the colt's sleek mane when he heard Tug bark joyfully. Looking through the stall window he saw Bud Martin and his father outside.

Hartley Martin had a newspaper in his hand.

"Did you see this morning's *Courier?*" he asked Yance. "News about an old friend of ours. Here it is— just a little paragraph on page three. It says Harko Dan broke out of jail night before last."

Yance's black brows drew together in a frown.

"Harko Dan!" he muttered. "I thought we'd seen the last o' him. Any chance o' their catchin' him?"

"I talked to Chief Rooney—met him at the gate on the way in. He says the state's got a reward out for him, but he doesn't seem to think Harko Dan is dangerous.

Too old. He must be over sixty by now."

Yance shook his head and his mouth was grim. "He'll be dangerous as long as he lives," he said quietly. "Gypsies don't forget. I'll feel better when he's back behind bars."

"Well, keep your eye peeled," said Mr. Martin. "He's probably lying low somewhere, but there's always a chance he might show up here at the Fair. He never could keep away from horses."

Bud opened the stall door and greeted Shad. "Golly!" he exclaimed. "You've got Redwood looking like a million dollars. What did you use—furniture polish?"

"No," Shad laughed. "Just elbow grease. I guess it's easy when they're in good condition. Anyhow, it's a lot of fun. If you think Redwood is slicked up, take a look at Cedar's Boy!"

Mr. Martin was inspecting the big horse and he seemed pleased with what he saw.

"You've got a pretty good groom here, Yance," he said. "By the way, Shad, I filled out a pass for you to use. Have any trouble getting in this morning?"

"Not when I mentioned your name," the boy grinned. "Thanks a lot." And he put the paper carefully in his pocket.

Hartley Martin was running a knowing hand up and down the bay pacer's legs. "No trouble there," he commented.

"No," said Yance. "He's sound as a nut."

"How's he working? Think we ought to put him in anything before the Granite State Stakes?"

"He's ready to go any time. I'd say it wouldn't hurt him to start in that two-fourteen pace on Wednesday. But if you'd rather save him for the big one, it's up to you."

"Well, you'll be driving Redwood in the Juvenile Stakes Wednesday, and the mare's in the two-twenty trot tomorrow. Let's keep Cedar's Boy out till the big race and bring him up to it just right. Heard any more about entries for the Granite State?"

Yance nodded. "It's going to be a good field," he said. "At least two Grand Circuit horses that I know of, and some others that'll bear watching. I saw Joe Campbell's Mischief Direct working out this morning. They say she's the fastest pacer in the State o' Maine, an' she looks like she could step."

His boss grinned. "That's fine," he said. "We've got one that can step, too. Just ease him along so he's at top form Saturday. Think you'll need Shad for the next hour or two?"

"No," said Yance. "He's done a good morning's work."

Mr. Martin put a couple of dollar bills in Bud's hand. "You boys haven't had a chance to do the Fair," he remarked. "Go ahead and see the sights. I'll meet you here before race time."

.   .   .

Noon of opening day! The sun was bright but a fine westerly breeze kept the heat from being oppressive, and the flags billowed out gaily from their staffs. Crowds and noise filled the grounds, for somewhere between thirty thousand and forty thousand people were milling up and down the Midway, thronging through the exhibition buildings and bringing box lunches from their cars in the big parking lot. The vendors of balloons, peanuts, popcorn and crackerjack were yelling themselves hoarse. Barkers with megaphones and loud-speakers tried to outdo each other in catching the public's attention. Over all the din blared the music of the steam organ on the biggest merry-go-round.

"Great, isn't it?" asked Bud, shouting to make himself heard. "I guess there's nothing else to touch a real county fair!"

"Have you seen any side shows yet?" Shad inquired as they neared the Midway.

"Not yet. Let's take in a few, soon as we've had something to eat."

They were opposite the tent that featured Ki-Ko, the Wild Man, and the spieler was just getting wound up. Wearing a loud checked suit and gray derby hat, he stood on the platform and waved an arm toward the iron-barred cage beside him.

"KI-KO!" he roared. "KI-KO, the Wild Man—cap•
tured alive in the island o' Borneo by United States
Marines o' the Fifteenth Regiment! Hi! Hi! He's alive!
He's fierce! He's dangerous! They're just about to feed
him the raw meat!"

Standing on tiptoe to look over the heads of the
crowd, the boys could see a shaggy creature covered
with reddish hair that looked like an animal's pelt. It
crouched in a corner of the cage and made ferocious
gestures toward the onlookers. A shirt-sleeved man
stood outside the bars, poking at the captive with a
pitchfork and holding up a huge, unappetizing chunk
of raw beef.

"Yuh wanna see KI-KO fed?" cried the barker. "Yuh
wanna watch him tear the raw meat with his terrible
fangs? Right inside, folks—on'y a dime—the tenth part
of a dollar! Hi! Hi! He's alive!"

The tent flap was lifted and the keeper rolled the
cage back inside, brandishing his pitchfork all the
while.

"Hur-ry! Hur-ry!" screamed the showman. "They're
just about to feed him the raw meat. So step right this
way! Don't crowd, folks. That's it—a dime—ten cents
is all it costs to see KI-KO, the Wild Man!"

The boys made no move to follow the pushing customers into the tent.

"Got a new wild man this year," Shad remarked.

"This one isn't as fat as the one they used to have. Wonder what became o' the old geezer. Drank himself to death, I guess."

Bud laughed. "Wouldn't be surprised. I heard he used to work at the livery stable when he wasn't traveling with the show or doing time at the County Farm. Here's a wienie stand. Let's get a couple o' red hots."

In the crowd in front of the booth Shad spotted Hank and 'Poleon, and a few minutes later all four of the boys were munching hot dogs as they strolled up the Midway.

Hank was carrying a brightly lacquered cane and swinging it with an air. "I was tryin' for one o' those pearl-handled six-guns in the Hoop-La game," he explained. "But they're all-fired hard to put a ring over. This is what I got instead. Boy, you should've seen 'Poleon pitchin' baseballs at Duke, the Dodger! He beaned the poor guy four times in a row!"

'Poleon strutted proudly as he pulled a handful of cigars out of his pocket. "Here's what I won," he said. "I'll take 'em home to my ol' man. They're prob'ly stinkeroos, but he won't mind."

Shad pointed over toward the Mermaid tent. "Any of you fellows seen that one?" he asked.

"Nope," said Hank. "I heard a guy say it was no good. They seem to have a crowd around, though. Want to take a look?"

On the platform below the picture of the gorgeous

Nellie, a spieler was rattling off a string of adjectives describing the attractions of mermaids in general and this one in particular. He was a weasel-faced individual in a sport shirt, and his shifty eyes kept searching the crowd while he whined his extravagant phrases.

"Let's go in," said Bud. "Might as well be a sucker once. Here—I've got a dollar left that my dad gave me. I'll treat."

They pushed their way into the stuffy interior of the tent and up to the ropes that surrounded the exhibit. What they saw was a considerable shock, even to boys who knew the ways of side shows.

Shad's jaw dropped as he stared at the "only real mermaid in captivity."

In a small glass tank, filled with evil-smelling liquid, floated the body of a repulsive creature about three feet long. It was a mottled yellow-brown in color, and while its tail bore some resemblance to that of a fish, its forward part was far from human. Instead of arms a pair of flippers dangled at its sides. The head was a misshapen knob with a huge, blubbery upper lip, divided by a deep cleft.

"Ugh!" muttered Hank. "It's a mess, all right. But what is it?"

Bud wrinkled his nose. "Well, it's no mermaid, that's sure," he said. "I've got a hunch it's a manatee—a sea cow—dead and pickled. What a gyp!"

There were perhaps twenty other customers around

the tank, all peering in gloomy wonder at the gruesome
thing it contained. Glancing up, Shad saw a thickset
man detach himself from the group of onlookers and
tiptoe toward a heavy curtain at the rear of the tent.
In a single quick motion he lifted the edge of the
drapery and disappeared.

The boy nudged Bud, who was standing next to him.
"Did you see that?" he whispered. "There must be
something going on back there. Maybe that's where
they've got the real mermaid."

"Well, let's find out," said Bud. He beckoned to the
other boys and the four of them went quietly to the
rear of the tent. A sound of low voices came to them
through the thick folds of cloth.

Bud's hand pulled the curtain aside and Shad got a
glimpse of a canvas-walled room, cloudy with tobacco
smoke. Five or six men were sitting or standing around
a rough board table. On it were bottles, a dog-eared
book and several piles of money in coin and bills.

The men looked up, scowling at the intruders. One
of them pushed back his chair and strode toward them.

"What's the idea?" he growled. "Can't yuh see it's
private back here? You punks better scram quick, before you get hurt."

Bud stood his ground. "We took a look at your rot-
ten mermaid," he replied. "It was so bad we thought
maybe the real show was in here."

"Well, think again, kid," snapped one of the other

men. "Yuh heard what he told yuh. Take a powder—an' fast!"

They were all on their feet now and advancing ominously toward the boys. Hank and 'Poleon had already started for the main entrance. Bud and Shad backed out after them, letting the curtain fall into place. In another moment they were out among the swirling crowds of the Midway once more.

"Well!" said Hank. "That was a fine gang o' thugs."

Bud was rubbing his chin, looking thoughtful. 'Poleon's eyes blazed and his fists were clenched. "For two bits," he said, "I'd ha' busted that gorilla in the nose!"

"Wait a minute!" Shad exclaimed. "I've got it—that money on the table! Suppose they're taking bets on the races?"

"Gee," said Bud, "I believe you're right! Wish I'd got a closer look at that ledger they had. No wonder they were in a hurry to get us out o' there. Bookmaking's against the law."

"What do you think we ought to do about it?" asked Shad. "Tell the police?"

Hank shook his head. "No cop would listen to a bunch o' kids," he said. "Let's wait. Maybe we can get some real proof."

"I wonder," Bud mused. "Do you think you could recognize any of that crowd if you saw 'em again?"

"Sure. Why not?" said 'Poleon. "There was that heavy-set feller in the green sport shirt. I could spot his ugly mug anywhere. And the two taller ones, dark an' slick-haired—they looked like big city gangsters to me—the kind you see in the movies."

"They were tough birds, all right," Bud agreed. "But what about the little, thin chap that stayed back by the table? There was something queer about him. He looked real old, an' yet his hair was coal-black. He kept pretty much out of sight but I did get one look at his face and it was weird—pale and gray as putty!"

"I noticed that, too," Shad nodded. "He acted as if he wasn't anxious to have anybody see him."

The boys agreed to keep their eyes open, particularly around the track. If the gang in the mermaid tent were gamblers that seemed a likely place for their activities. After a few more minutes of sight-seeing, Shad left the others and went back to his job at the stable.

FIVE

THE crowds were all heading in one direction now. Dust rose in a haze from the scuffing of thousands of feet, moving toward the track and the grandstand. In the infield pavilion, just behind the judges' stand, the Riverdale Silver Cornet Band was tuning up with a shrilling of trumpets and a booming blare of oompah horns.

It gave Shad a happy feeling just to look and listen. The first race would be called in half an hour! A tingle of excitement ran through his veins and he sprinted the last hundred yards to the stables.

He wormed his way through a milling crowd of horsemen into the center of activity. Trainers and swipes were putting last-minute touches on the dozen sleek trotters that stood in the harnessing enclosure. Fresh bandages were being wrapped around slender forelegs, and kneepads carefully adjusted. A horseshoer was tightening the hind plates on a fretful little black mare.

Over by the fence lounged the drivers, aloof and taciturn. Most of them were lean, hard-bitten men of middle age, wearing their colorful silks and tight moleskin pants with careless ease. Goggles were pushed up on their full-crowned, floppy caps. Some chewed tobacco

and some held the cold stumps of cigars gripped in the corners of their mouths, but there was a look about all their faces that was alike—the unmistakable, weather-tanned stamp of the harness track.

When he reached his own stable, Shad found Yance sitting on a feedbox, talking to a wrinkled, brown-faced old man with merry blue eyes. The gypsy beckoned to him.

"Shad," he said, "I want you to meet Billy Randall. He's the best trainer in the business, bar none. Retired now, but still tops, far's I'm concerned."

The old fellow's calloused hand took Shad's in an iron grip.

"Don't believe all Yance tells ye," he grinned. "He's a mite prejudiced, 'cause I learnt him a few tricks. Hear ye got a hankerin' to work with hosses, son."

"I guess I like it better'n anything else in the world," the boy admitted shyly.

Randall nodded and gave him a long, slow look of appraisal. "Mebbe ye got what it takes," he said. "Some men can talk to a horse with their voice, an' some with their hands. Drivin', I'd say the men with hands had the edge, but it don't hurt none if ye have both."

"Shad hasn't done any driving yet," Yance put in, "but he's got Cedar's Boy an' Redwood so they trust him as much as they do me.

"Tell you what, Shad," he went on. "You go watch the first three races. I'd just as soon stay here an' talk to Billy. There's a couple o' horses in the fourth an' fifth I want to see, because I'll be driving against 'em later in the week, so you go ahead an' be back here after the finish o' the third race."

Shad needed no urging. Within two minutes he was wriggling through the crowd that jammed the entrance to the grandstand. Not that he was going to pay half a dollar for a seat. No indeed—the place he had picked for himself was across the track, in the infield.

Right ahead of him, as he made for the fence, he heard a loud commotion. Standing on tiptoe he could see a thin, elderly man with a beard and a mane of white hair. The old fellow's eyes stared wildly and he

waved his arms as if he were trying to hold back the
tide of people pushing toward the stands. In his hand
was a tattered Bible.

"Doom!" he screamed, in a high, cracked voice.
"The doom of the ungodly is upon you! Harken to the
voice of the prophet: 'Woe to the bloody city! It is all
full of lies and robbery. The noise of the whip, and the
noise of the rattling of the wheels and of the prancing
horses!' That's from the third chapter of Nahum, first
and second verses. If you don't believe the words of
Holy Writ, look at me an' be warned! I was saved out
o' the snare—snatched like a brand from the burning!
Horses is sin, folks, an' all of you who rejoice in the
racing of horses is doomed to roast in eternal fire!"

The people laughed in the old fellow's face and
shoved on past him toward the grandstand entrance.
Shad knew the man must be crazy but he was so earnest
in his crusade that it was hard not to feel a kind of
sympathy for him. Long after the gaunt figure was lost
in the throng of race-goers his yells of warning still
rang out above all the noises of the track.

Shad ducked under the fence and darted across the
carefully leveled earth of the straightaway. Hundreds
of people, including many of the stable hands, were
already finding places along the rail of the infield. The
boy took his position about a hundred yards from the
finish line. There he could watch the drivers turning
to score, and get a good view up the stretch.

The stands were filling fast now. Sellers of peanuts, bottled pop and ice cream scurried up and down the aisles calling their wares, but soon their shouts were drowned out by a burst of music. The American flag was hoisted to the top of the staff as the band played the national anthem.

Hardly had the last notes faded and the people resumed their seats when the starter's voice brayed out over the loud-speaker.

"Calling drivers for the first race," it intoned. "All out for the two-twenty-four trot. Get your horses out here, gentlemen."

As Shad knew enough to expect, that first call brought no action—at least, none that was visible from the track. The starter and the judges kept on chatting in their little stand. The band broke into a lively march tune and the spectators bought more pop and peanuts. After a few minutes the call was repeated.

This time there was activity at the mouth of the chute. A big bay trotter came walking out, led by a groom. His head was down, relaxed and easy, as he sniffed at the smooth surface of the track. Between his ears, like a plume, rose the oval plate that bore his number—the figure 1—repeated in larger size on his saddle cloth.

Shad had found a score card dropped by the rail, and now he looked up the horse's name. "No. 1," he read, "Firehouse Guy, b.g., 2.11⅕, driver, K. M.

Wicks."

Ken Wicks. Shad remembered him from other years as a seasoned reinsman who generally won his share of purses. The big bay gelding was new to the track but Shad liked his name and his looks. From that moment he was pulling for Firehouse Guy.

Wicks strolled out behind the sulky, trailing his whip. He fastened the bay's checkrein, gathered the lines and swung into the seat. Then, with heels settled in the stirrups, he took his horse down the stretch at a jog.

By that time others were on the track—five, six, finally nine of them—a big field. They warmed up briefly and came straggling back past the judges' stand under a rapid fire of comment from the starter. His voice blared loud over the amplifier:

"Come on, Jarvis, get that mare steadied down . . . not too far, Wicks—remember, you've got the pole . . . pick that horse up, Number Five, and find your position."

They turned, halfway up the stretch and, with the horses all headed the same way, some sort of order appeared. Five sulkies were strung out in a ragged line across the track, with four more in the second row.

"All right," yelled the starter. "Bring 'em down, an' let's see how you look."

Shad didn't need the clang of the bell to tell him it was no start as they swept past the stand. At least three horses were out of position. The second score was little better, and the starter was growing sarcastic. They got away at last on their third try and swung into the lower turn well bunched.

Shad pivoted, watching them move up the back-stretch. On the upper turn he saw that Firehouse Guy still had the pole position. A brown mare, trotting hard, was coming up on the outside and the rest were trailing. As they rounded into the straightaway the rhythmic thunder of their hoofs grew in volume and Shad's heart beat faster. This was the music he loved best in all the world.

The mare pulled abreast as they passed the stand, but Wicks kept the big horse steady, and they were still nose to nose at the foot of the stretch. It was a two-horse race now and the crowd began to roar its approval. Up the far side of the track they went like a matched pair. Jarvis was plying his whip over the little mare as they made the last turn, and Shad saw her inching to the front, flattened out and trotting with all she had.

"Wheel lock!" yelled a man at his side. "The mare's got him now!"

The two trotters were crowded close to the fence as they pounded down the straightaway, and Shad could see Jarvis leaning to the left, bending the springy sulky frame so that it overlapped the fork on Wicks' right wheel.

Wicks shouted something at the other driver, then cut down with his whip on the big bay's flank. There was a screech of steel as Firehouse Guy responded. The mare's sulky wheel lifted a foot off the ground and for a breathless instant it seemed as if it must tip over. Then Jarvis righted himself. The brown mare was thrown off stride by the wrench of the sulky shaft. She broke into a gallop, and Firehouse Guy, trotting like a steam engine, came under the wire a winner.

Jarvis was white-faced and angry when they brought their horses back to the judges' stand. He tried to claim he had been fouled, but the wise old horsemen in the box merely smiled and shook their heads. Wicks took the heat and the mare was disqualified for breaking in the stretch.

The second mile was an anticlimax, for Firehouse Guy got off fast and stayed well in front through both laps. Timed in 2.14 for the first heat, he captured the second in an easy 2.20 to take the winner's end of a $500 purse.

As he waited for the start of the next race, Shad heard two men talking in the crowd along the infield fence. Their voices were low and cautious, but the word or two he caught made him edge nearer.

"Sure," one of them was murmuring. "Five dollars on the nose. At three to one I've got fifteen comin'. Guess I'll mosey over an' collect."

"Lemme go along," the other replied. "I'd sort o'

like to get somethin' down on Bluebell in the fourth.
You can tell 'em I'm okay."

They went off in the direction of the Midway, and
Shad followed at a discreet distance. He kept them in
sight until they entered the side show tent where the
"mermaid" was on display. Then he hurried back to
the track, so excited by his discovery that he found it
hard to concentrate on the trotters.

He watched the shifting crowds across the track and
in the stands, hoping to spot one of his friends. But
it was not until the third race ended that he caught a
glimpse of Bud Martin and his father standing near the
ticket window. He sprinted across the straightaway
and grabbed Bud's arm.

"Got a minute?" he whispered. "I think I've got a
lead on those guys."

The other boy followed him a few steps, till they
could talk in private, and Shad told him about the
conversation he had overheard.

"I trailed 'em straight to the mermaid tent," he concluded. "That's pretty good evidence, wouldn't you
think?"

"Sure it is," said Bud. "No question about it—they're
running a bookie hangout. Let's tell Dad the whole
thing. He knows Chief Rooney, an' the police would
believe him a lot quicker'n they would us."

They returned to the place where they had left Mr.
Martin, but he was no longer there.

"Maybe he went back to the stable," said Shad. "I've got to go anyhow. I promised Yance I'd come back after the third race. If your father's there I'll tell him."

When the boy reached the stable he found nobody but Yance. The gypsy trainer heard his story without surprise.

"That's right," he said. "There's always betting going on under cover. Guess you can't have a horse race without some o' that. If one crowd gets pinched, another gang takes over. It won't hurt to tell Mr. Martin if you see him, but all the cops in the state couldn't keep a few dollars from changing hands."

He gave Shad some brief instructions, patted Tug's white head and went off to watch the rest of the afternoon's racing. The boy could hear the drumming of hoofbeats from the track and the steady clamor that rose from the stands. Restless, he tried to find jobs to occupy him. While the bull terrier sat by and watched him work, he took down one set of shining harness after another and touched up imaginary spots of dirt with saddle soap.

He wondered how his mother was making out with her apple pie. Tomorrow would be the big day for the food exhibits, with the judging to take place at noon. The reason for that hour, he had been told, was to make sure that the judges approached their pleasant task with good appetites.

When he had finished the harness he went to the

end stall and looked in at Sequoia. The sorrel mare
whinnied softly and tossed her pretty head, eager for
attention. Her glossy coat showed no special need of
grooming but he brought the currycomb and brush
and went in anyway, just to get acquainted.

She seemed to enjoy every caressing stroke of the
brush. As he talked to her gently and called her pet
names she answered with little nods of her head and
flicks of her long, honey-colored tail.

He was kneeling to put the last touches on her trim
ankles when he heard Tug growl outside. Rising
quickly he went to the stall door. The white terrier
stood with legs braced and hackles up, looking past
the north end of the stable. Shad picked up a pitchfork and moved quietly along beneath the overhanging shed roof. At the corner by the tack room he

paused, thinking he heard a board creak.

"Go get 'em, Tug!" he whispered, and the dog raced past him, heading for the fence behind the stable. Shad gripped the fork and followed.

There was no one in sight. However, Tug was sniffing at a board in the fence, and as he came closer Shad realized it was at the very spot where he and his companions had made their entrance on Saturday. He listened and thought he heard a sound of scrambling, far down the bank toward the river.

"Hey—Hank!" he called. " 'Poleon!"

He waited several seconds but there was no answer. Whoever it was who had caused Tug's growling, he knew it wasn't his friends.

SIX

OLD Billy Randall was with Yance when he came back after the last race. The white-haired trainer walked with a limp, Shad noticed.

They were talking busily and the boy didn't want to interrupt, so he said nothing about what had happened in their absence.

"Did ye see ol' Jeremiah Jones?" Randall asked with a chuckle. "He's still preachin' fire an' brimstone fer us lost souls that follers the hosses!"

"I saw him," Shad put in. "Is there something wrong with him?"

"Cracked as a busted teapot," said the old man. He shook his head pityingly. "Jerry allus used to hang around the hoss-tracks, an' one time he was a pretty fair driver, so they say. Then he got to plungin' heavy with the bookmakers. Mortgaged about ever'thin' he owned to make a killin' on one race, an' when his hoss won he stood to collect thousan's o' dollars. But the

bookie skipped the country. That done it. Somethin'
went haywire in poor Jerry's head. Ever since he's
been goin' around warnin' folks they're doomed, an'
quotin' scripture to prove hosses is the main cause o'
man's downfall."

"If he hates horses so much," said Shad, "I should
think he'd be dangerous to have around."

"Oh, I reckon he's harmless enough," the old trainer
replied. "The boys tell me ye seen a slick piece o'
drivin' in that first heat today, son."

"You mean Ken Wicks?" asked Shad. "Gee—I'll say!
Jarvis thought he had him with a frame lock, but he
broke it, pretty as you please."

Randall grinned approvingly. "Takes a big, strong
hoss to pull a trick like that," he said, "an' one with a
sudden turn o' speed. I've seen both sulkies piled up
an' the hosses an' drivers hurt when a feller tried to
bust out of a frame lock. Generally all ye can do is
drop back an' give him the lead."

For an hour Shad sat on an overturned water bucket
listening with all his ears. With Yance to prompt him,
the old man rambled on about horses he had trained
and races he had driven.

"I was just a greenhorn kid when I drove my first
heat on the Roarin' Grand," he said. "That was at a
mile track in Ohio. 'Most fifty year ago. An' guess who
was in that race. Only Pop Geers an' Walter Cox, that's
all! Prob'ly the two best men that ever sat on a hoss's

tail. I was up behind a good, fast colt but they made me look mighty silly. First heat I guess I took 'em by surprise. Stole the pole goin' up the backstretch an' brought my hoss home ahead in a tight finish, with Geers second.

"They was layin' for me in the next heat. Pop went to the whip early an' got the pole, with my colt breathin' right down his neck. When I started to pull out for a pass, there was Cox huggin' my wheel. Nothin' I tried did me a bit o' good. I was boxed for sure.

"Well, sir, I wasn't goin' to let 'em do that to me again. Come time for the third heat I brought the colt down too fast an' he broke, goin' into the first turn. When I got him trottin' again, the whole field had passed me, an' Geers was out ahead by five lengths. I pulled to the outside an' sent the colt after 'em, flattened out an' goin' like the wind. By the time we hit the last turn there was nobody ahead but Geers an' Cox. I thought I could pass 'em, but the wider I went on the curve, the less room I had. Cox just edged out enough to hold me without gettin' caught at it by the judges. Comin' down the stretch the colt was finished, an' I hadn't the heart to drive him. Pop Geers took the heat an' the race. Fetch me a dipper o' water, son. I'm dry, talkin' so much."

Shad ran to get it for him, afraid he might miss a word. When Randall had gulped down the drink and wiped his mouth on the back of his hand, the boy ventured a question.

"Did you ever beat 'em—after that time, I mean?"

"Not Pop Geers. Guess he was always too smart for me, or his hosses was too fast. But I took Walter into camp a few times. Once, I recollect, was in the big fall Grand Circuit meetin' down in the Bluegrass, at Lexin'ton. That was the year I raced ol' Cedar. Cox had a flashy sidewheeler that had taken a lot o' purses, an' we was both entered in the two-ten pace.

"He gave me odds o' three to one," the old driver chuckled. "When I come back home I brought my wife a new fur coat."

"How'd you beat him?" asked Shad. "Any tricks?"

Randall snorted. "Not a single trick," said he. "Jes' plain speed. Cedar paced the legs off that nag in straight heats. He set a track record that day—two-two-an'-a-half for two heats in a row."

"What kind of a horse was Cedar to drive?" asked Yance. "I was too young to handle him in a race."

"He was about ideal," Randall replied thoughtfully. "You know there's all kinds o' harness hosses, just as there's all kinds o' folks. Some is kind an' some mean. Some is plain stupid an' a few is too smart for their own good. Take a smart hoss that thinks he knows more'n you do an' you're bound to get in trouble.

"But ol' Cedar—he wasn't jes' smart—he was sensible. Once he trusted his driver he'd do what you told him an' no questions asked. Had a nice mouth. He could feel what you wanted through the reins. An' when you wanted him to go, my golly, how he could put out! He got his natural style an' speed from Caribou, his sire. But more'n that he had plenty o' heart. That come from ol' Betsy, his dam. She wasn't so fast, but she was a Morgan from 'way back, an' that means grit clean through."

"How do you tell a horse what you want?" asked Shad. "With your hands, I mean—through the reins?"

The old man looked at him with a twinkle in his eyes. "Son," he said, "if that was somethin' could be told in words, anybody could be a good race driver. But it ain't. If you've got it, the hoss knows by the touch o' the lines an' the feel o' the bit in his mouth. An' you know by the way he answers—the way he steadies down for you, or lays out to trot with all he's got. There ain't no teacher can give it to you. Gotta be born with it."

"Gee," Shad breathed. "I'd sure like to try."

Yance stood up and stretched. "Well," he said, "if you get up early enough, maybe you'll have a chance. I was thinkin' I'd let you exercise Redwood in the mornin'."

Shad's eyes popped wide and he could find no words to answer. He wondered how he would be able to wait till tomorrow's sunrise.

It was growing dark over the Fair Grounds now, and the lights on the big Ferris wheel glittered like a string of jewels. Ordinarily Shad would have felt an urge to rush off and mingle with the crowds on the bright Midway, but tonight he was content to stay right here.

Yance struck a match for Randall's cigar and the old trainer went on talking.

"There's only a few of us oldtimers left," he said. "Half a dozen, maybe. By oldtimers, I mean the fellers that remember back to the high-wheel sulky an' the first mile under two-ten. I was just a kid in knee-pants but I ain't likely to forget the day we got the news from Cleveland that Maud S. had trotted in two-eight-an'-three-quarters against time. That was in July, 1885 —the fastest mile a hoss had ever gone in harness up to then. I reckon if old Maud S. had been hitched to one of our modern racin' bikes she could've knocked another five or six seconds off her record."

The end of his cigar glowed red in the darkness. "Them was the days," he continued, "when folks was just findin' out what breedin' could do for speed. The big farms in 'York State an' Kentucky was usin' sons an' grandsons of old Hambletonian for sires, an' crossin' 'em with the famous Clay mares like American Girl an' Lucy. The colts they got wasn't only fast but handsome. That was the start o' the real standardbred hoss —the kind you see on every track in the country today.

"Up to then most folks thought it would harm a colt to race him before he was four years old. Why,

I've heard Goldsmith Maid was six before they ever strapped leather on her, an' eight when she started to race. Then along come Leland Stanford, out in California, an' started a whale of a big breedin' farm. He decided to hitch his colts an' fillies right to a sulky before they was two an' let 'em grow up in harness. An' durned if it didn't work!

"When Stanford's mare Sunol was a three-year-old she trotted a mile in two-ten-an'-a-half. Along in the nineties there was more an' more youngsters comin' up that could trot as fast as the older hosses. Pretty soon we begun to have reg'lar three-year-old races on the Grand Circuit, an' even Futurities for two-year-olds.

"We was gettin' better-built tracks by then," he said, "an' that helped bring the records down. But the biggest change of all was the rubber-tired, ball-bearin' sulky. I bet you didn't know this, Yance, but it was

Ed Geers himself that drove the first race in the new contraption. That's a fact. The feller that built it—man name of Elliot, here in New England—sent it out to Detroit for Budd Doble to try in 1892. Doble turned up his nose at it at first. Told Geers he could use it. Pop told me that when he come out on the track with his hoss hitched to that thing, you could ha' heard the crowd laughin' clear over in Canada. He won his race, though, an' Doble grabbed the sulky back mighty quick. From then on the bike builders couldn't turn 'em out fast enough."

The old man's eyes closed for a few seconds, and only the brightening and fading disk of his cigar showed that he was awake.

"I've seen 'em all in my time," he went on at last. "All the good 'uns in fifty years o' racin'. I've seen the Peter the Great colts an' the Axworthy colts wipe most o' the others right off the map. I was down to Readville with my dad the day Star Pointer paced the first mile ever done under two minutes. I saw Lou Dillon an' Dan Patch an' the Harvester when they was top o' the world, an' so on right down to Dean Hanover an' Billy Direct."

He sighed. "When I helped Sep Palin train ol' Greyhound," he said, "I knew I was lookin' at the greatest of 'em all. Don't expect I'll live to see the trotter that can beat his record o' one-fifty-five-an'-a-quarter. But you will, sonny"—he pointed his finger at Shad—"you'll see a colt come along some day an' do it."

At that moment Tug growled. Listening, Shad thought he could hear footsteps above the distant sound of the crowds and the music that came from the Midway. Then two figures appeared in the darkness.

"That you, Shad?" asked a familiar voice.

"Yeah, 'Poleon," he replied. "Right this way. Come here, Tug, an' be quiet."

As the bull terrier obeyed, Hank Wetherbee and 'Poleon Doucette came to an awkward halt, shy at finding themselves in the presence of the older men.

Shad introduced them. "How's the Fair going?" he asked.

"Nothin' wrong with the Fair," said Hank. "We've had about all of it we can take for one day, though, an' now we're tryin' to get home. Any idea what became o' the boat?"

"The boat?" asked Shad blankly. "Why—isn't it

where you left it?"

'Poleon shook his head. "We tied it down there in the reg'lar place," he said. "When we went to get it, a few minutes ago, it was gone."

"Wait!" Shad exclaimed. "I'd 'most forgotten. Back about five o'clock there was somebody around behind the stable. Tug made a fuss an' I went out to look. I thought I'd heard a noise back by the fence, but by the time I got there they'd gone on down the bank. Whoever that was must have swiped the boat."

"Doggone it," Hank muttered. "I bet it's Joe Dubois an' that bunch o' kids from Squantic. They've been snoopin' around tryin' to find out our secret way o' gettin' into the Fair. Well, 'Poleon, looks like we'll have to walk home, or take the bus."

Shad grinned. "That's tough," he said, "but you'll find the boat all right in the morning. If it was Joe Dubois who took it he won't have sense enough to hide it. So long. See you tomorrow."

Billy Randall got up stiffly and hobbled after them. "Time I was gettin' along, too," he said. "Good night, all."

Shad waited till the old trainer was well out of hearing. "Gee," he said, "he's great, isn't he?"

"One o' the best," Yance replied.

"How'd he get that limp? Was it a racing accident?"

"No," said Yance. "He got stomped on by a crazy stallion. Busted his leg in three places. Lucky the horse didn't kill him."

The gypsy stretched his arms and yawned. "I aim to have Cedar's Boy on the track at five, so I guess I'd better turn in. You'd better, too. Get yourself an armful o' clean straw an' curl up there in the tack room."

Shad made himself a nest of sweet-smelling oat straw and lay down, pillowing his head on his arm. The sounds of the Fair were far enough away to blend into a soothing lullaby.

"Gosh," he smiled to himself drowsily. "Going to drive Redwood in the morning!" And then, before he knew it, he was fast asleep.

SEVEN

THE eastern sky was just beginning to gray when Shad woke. There was something cold chucking him under the chin, and when he opened his eyes he discovered it was Tug's moist nose. Over in the poultry building the prize roosters were crowing like mad, and in Cedar's Boy's stall, beyond the partition, he could hear sounds of harnessing.

Shad jumped up and ran to the water tap to wash his face. It was going to be another fine day—probably hot before it ended. He felt very hungry. After a moment's wondering he remembered that he had eaten no supper.

"How's your appetite?" asked Yance, as the boy put his head in the stall door.

"I'm starved," Shad grinned.

"We'll go over to the horsemen's boardinghouse soon's we've done our driving. With Billy Randall here last night I plumb forgot to eat."

Shad helped buckle the big red pacer between the shafts of the training cart and snapped the check-rein to the hook. The cart had bike wheels, like a sulky, and was almost as lightly built. The seat, however, was placed farther back, and a tiny dashboard protected the driver's face from flying dirt.

Yance strapped his stop watch in the palm of his left hand, settled his feet in the stirrups and nodded for Shad to let go the horse's head.

As Cedar's Boy went toward the track at his quick, long-striding pacer's walk, the boy followed part way. From the corner by the big stable building he could get a view of most of the half-mile oval and still keep an eye on his charges in their stalls. He wanted to see just how Yance did it.

Eager as the red horse had been for his workout, he seemed content to jog as long as he moved clockwise around the track. When his muscles loosened up, Shad could see him step out a little faster. But Yance kept him at a loafing gait for half a dozen laps, still headed the wrong way. Finally, as they passed the empty judges' stand and went up the stretch, Shad saw the driver slow the big pacer to a walk and turn him. With a snort of satisfaction, Cedar's Boy settled down to action. He came down to the wire easily but gaining speed with every stride.

Yance had pulled his goggles down to shield his eyes and was leaning forward, no longer slouching on the seat. Cedar's Boy was really going now. Shad held his breath as he watched the big bay flatten out and tear into the backstretch. Then, out of the corner of his eye he saw something else.

Crouching by the rail was a heavily built man in a green sport shirt. His glance kept shifting from the pacer on the track to something he held in his hand. Shad knew him instantly—the ugly-visaged bruiser who

LEE TOWNSEND

had been in the mermaid tent the day before. And he was clocking the red horse's time!

The boy moved back out of sight. He didn't think the man had seen him and he thought it would be better if he weren't recognized. Careful to keep the grandstand between him and the track, he went back to the stable. Yance would be coming in soon, and there was no harm in getting the harness on Redwood.

The colt was fidgety, eager to be out of his stall. Shad needed all his patience and gentleness to get the bit settled comfortably in Redwood's mouth and the crown-strap over his ears. He was just buckling the girth when the trainer returned with Cedar's Boy.

"That was a nice workout," said Yance. "I breezed him a half in close to a minute-an'-three."

"He sure looked good," Shad replied. "I watched the start of it. Did you notice anybody by the rail, when you came in?"

"Sure—a couple of other trainers. There were quite a few horses out when I left. Why?"

"I thought there was a clocker there," said Shad. "A heavy-set guy in a green shirt. I wouldn't have thought much about it only he was one o' those men we saw in the bookie hangout I was telling you about."

Yance frowned. "I guess he ducked while I was jogging the cool-out lap," he said. "Don't like the idea o' his clocking my horse, though. Looks like they were trying to get a line on Saturday's race."

The gypsy gave Shad a hand with the colt's harnessing and hooked up the traces to the training-cart.

"He'll want to go," he told the boy. "There'll be a lot of other horses on the track, so don't let him get to traveling too fast. Take him four or five laps the wrong way o' the track an' stay on the outside so you won't get in any trouble. When you think he's steadied down enough, turn him 'round an' let him move. I don't want any time trial—just a good breeze. Here— take my stop watch an' try to keep him at a three-minute gait—not under."

Proudly, Shad strapped the watch into his palm, where his thumb could reach the stop lever. He put on Yance's goggles, too, and climbed to the tiny seat, dropping his heels into the stirrups. The colt felt the vibration in the shafts and knew his driver was up. He reared and pranced, but Yance held his bridle, talking to him softly.

"All set?" he asked. "Okay, son, let's see if you're a driver."

Shad's heart was pounding but he grinned, trying to look nonchalant. He shortened his grip on the reins and lifted them an inch off the colt's back. And as Yance let go of the bridle, Redwood got under way. Pacing smoothly he pricked up his ears and headed for the track.

At the gate Shad had to pull him in sharply, for five trotters were coming down the straightaway, well bunched and moving fast. He waited till they had passed, then swung the colt to the left and let him out a little.

Intent as he was on his driving, the boy stole one glance at the rail, looking for the green-shirted clocker, but the man had disappeared. Apparently his only interest had been in the big bay horse.

Redwood was behaving well enough, though he tossed his head occasionally and reached farther than necessary with his forefeet. Shad kept his hands steady on the reins. He tried to pass on to the colt a calmness he didn't really feel. Then he began talking to him in a low, gentle voice. That worked better, and by the time they had made one circuit of the track his own nervousness was gone. With a thrill, he knew what old Billy Randall had been talking about. Obedient to his touch on the lines, the two-year-old was rocking along as smooth as silk.

The dust on the outer rim of the oval, where the sprinklers had not reached, was almost fetlock deep. It rose in clouds under the colt's feet and made Shad sneeze once or twice. He was glad to have his eyes protected by the goggles.

When he had counted five laps he waited for a clear track and turned Redwood near the head of the stretch. The young chestnut's ears pricked up sharply. Shad could feel the eagerness in his mouth as he tried to grab the bit.

"Easy, boy," he murmured. "This isn't a race. I'm s'posed to keep you over a minute an' a half for the lap."

As they passed the judges' stand the boy's thumb clicked the start on Yance's watch. He let Redwood out but had no need to urge him. The colt was breezing in perfect rhythm.

They went up the backstretch at the same fast, steady pace, hugging the inside rail. At the quarter post Shad glanced at the watch. Forty-seven seconds. He could afford to step it up a little. There was a trotter in a sulky just ahead and the boy swung Redwood wide to pass on the turn.

The other driver glanced up as he caught sight of the colt's head. He flicked the whip lightly over his big brown horse and the trotter pulled away. The competitive urge was too strong for Shad. The orders Yance had given him hadn't forbidden brushing, and Redwood wanted to go. He lifted the reins a little, took a firmer grip and let the young pacer out. In an instant Redwood's stride had lengthened and quickened. He had even more enthusiasm than his young driver for catching up with the big brown trotter.

Still going wide, they were less than a length behind as they completed the turn. The straightaway opened out clear in front of them. Shad had no whip, but he didn't need one. The colt, going beautifully, was already coming up again, abreast of the other sulky.

At that moment the boy heard an angry shout. Right ahead he saw a horse moving out through the gate onto the track. The driver sawed at his horse's mouth, yanking him toward the rail, and in a panic Shad pulled Redwood to the left. Fortunately he had been going so wide that he had room to maneuver, but it

was a close shave. His right wheel missed the wheel of the sulky coming toward him by inches.

Confused and frightened, the colt had lost the smoothness of his stride. He might have broken if Shad hadn't regained his own coolness.

"All right, boy," he said, trying to make his voice reassuring. "Steady, now. Nobody's hurt."

A derisive laugh came back from the driver of the brown trotter as his horse went under the wire. Shad gritted his teeth and pushed the stop lever of the watch. When he had Redwood slowed and calmed down, he looked at the time. One-twenty-three. He had

gone the last quarter in thirty-six seconds—a lot faster
than he had any business to. He was turning the colt
to take him off the track when the brown horse jogged
past. The driver looked at him with a leer that was
almost an insult, and spat in the direction of the colt's
heels. It was Jake Jarvis, the man who had been so
close to trouble in yesterday's race.

Angry for a moment, Shad had sobered by the time
he got back to the stable. Yance looked the colt over
carefully and seemed satisfied. "How'd he go?" he
asked quietly.

"Fine," said Shad, and hesitated. "I—I let him go a
little faster'n I should have," he admitted. "Jake Jarvis
had a trotter out an' Redwood wanted to brush, so I
let him. We did the half in one-twenty-three."

Yance looked at him, poker-faced. "I know," he said.
"I saw the whole thing. That scrape by the gate wasn't
your fault, an' you got out of it in good shape. I'm
satisfied you can drive. Only next time I reckon you'll
stick to orders."

"I sure will," Shad promised, grateful that the
trainer had let him off so easily.

He walked Redwood up and down a while to cool
him out, then curried and brushed him till the lights
twinkled in his satin coat. Yance had finished grooming Cedar's Boy when Shad came out of the stall.

"You know what Redwood paced that last quarter
in?" Shad asked. "I got it at thirty-six seconds. An' that

included a near break at the end. Do you think he could keep that up for a mile?"

"Might," said Yance. "I don't want to push him in training, though. Remember—he's only a baby yet. A two-year-old. I'm a bit old-fashioned about taking too much out of a colt when he's so young. We'll see how he does in the Futurity tomorrow. That'll be his first race. Mr. Martin entered him more'n a year ago."

Shad had taken the stop watch off and put it in his pocket when he came in from the track. Now he handed it to Yance. "Hope you'll let me wear that every morning," he grinned.

The trainer nodded. "You'll be driving him or Sequoia regular," he said, and glanced at the watch. "Well, it's six-thirty. What do you say if we eat?"

It had been an hour since the boy had even thought about food. Now he remembered how hungry he was and his mouth began to water. The few hundred yards they walked to the frame building beyond the stables seemed like a mile.

Their breakfast at the boardinghouse was all that any hungry boy could ask. He had a big bowl of corn flakes and a banana, followed by sausages, fried potatoes and flapjacks with real New Hampshire maple syrup. By the time he got up from the table he was full almost to bursting.

At the door, Yance filled his pipe and lighted it. He greeted some of the other grooms and trainers coming in for their morning meal. One of them scowled at Shad and the boy recognized him as the driver who had come so near cracking him up.

"Punks like you oughta keep off the track," he muttered as he passed. Like a flash Yance moved around in front of him.

"You can thank this kid you're not in the hospital," he answered coldly. "You know the rules. Wait till you've got a clear track before you go through the gate. So keep a civil tongue in your head when you talk to a real driver."

The other man was half a head taller than Yance but he wilted under the gypsy's steady eye.

"Okay," he mumbled. "I didn't mean nothin'." And he sidled past into the dining room.

Yance was quiet as they returned to the stables, and Shad knew better than to do any talking. He helped the trainer harness Sequoia.

"Tell you what," said Yance, when the last strap was buckled. "Just to show I trust your driving, I'm going to let you take the mare out. Here's the watch. Let's see if you can jog her six times 'round, an' then turn in a good, clean two-twenty-four mile. I want the first lap in one-fifteen. The second, you can really let her go. She'll give you one-nine or better."

Shad set his jaw. "Yes, sir," he said, and climbed into the sulky. He was sitting on the sorrel's long tail, and his widespread feet were right up alongside her hindquarters. He was so close that he felt almost like a part of the trotter. Now he knew what drivers meant when they talked about having horses "in their laps."

The track was empty at the moment. He adjusted his goggles and took her the three slow miles Yance had specified. By the time he turned for the time trial there were two or three other sulkies out, but he came down to the line at a good clip.

Sequoia was an old hand at this business. She knew exactly what was wanted and her clean-muscled legs moved like pistons. Shad, trying to judge her speed, thought the mare was going about right. He held the reins lightly and let her do it her own way.

At the end of the first half-mile he looked at the watch. One-fifteen, right on the nose.

"All right, lady," he told the mare, "let's go!"

She felt the difference in the way he held the reins, and it was a joy to watch her back flatten as she stretched her stride. The wind screamed louder in Shad's ears. He kept Sequoia close to the pole as they rounded the curve and stormed up the backstretch. There was nothing in front of them, but even without the spur of competition the mare needed no driving. She trotted for the sheer love of it.

At the finish line, Shad was a full second late in remembering the stop watch. But it showed two-twenty-three!

"Gee," he told Yance, when he brought the mare

in, "she sure is a sweetheart to drive! Must ha' done that last half at a two-fifteen clip."

The gypsy grinned. "You did all right," he said. "Soon as you've dried her out an' curried her you can take some time off."

"Thanks, Yance," said the boy. "I can use it. My Ma's got a pie entered in the cookery exhibit, an' I'd kind o' like to be there."

EIGHT

WHEN he entered the Home Products Building, at eleven-thirty, he was glad he'd eaten a big breakfast. Otherwise the sight and smell of so much tempting food would have set him crazy.

The place was jammed with people—mostly womenfolk. A fair number of sheepish-looking husbands and a throng of hungry boys and girls were also present. The judges were already working down the line of jellies, preserves and pickles. Baked goods would come next.

Shad located his mother after a few minutes. As he had expected, she was standing near enough to the pie table to keep an eye on her handiwork, but far enough away so that nobody would suspect her of having a proprietary interest. Her stern face broke into a smile as she caught sight of him.

"Well, Melvin," she said, "you look better'n I thought you might—sleeping in the hay and all. I see you even remembered to wash behind your ears."

Shad flushed under her inspection. "Gosh, Ma, folks are looking at us," he murmured. "Sure, I washed plenty, an' combed my hair an' everything. How'd your pie turn out? Did you get the Greenings?"

Mrs. Davis nodded and pursed her lips. "It's hard to tell what the judges'll think," she said with a little frown. "A lot depends on the spices. I used fresh cinnamon an' grated my own nutmeg. The crust's tender enough, an' browned just right. Your father thought the other pie I baked at the same time was perfect, but o' course he's partial to my cooking."

"Which one is it?" asked Shad.

She glanced sidelong at the table and spoke in a whisper. "Third one from the left on the front row."

The boy walked slowly past the exhibit and came back to join her. He gave her a reassuring grin.

"Best-looking pie in the bunch," he told her. "That card—'Mrs. Myron Davis'—makes me feel mighty proud."

She patted his arm. "You're a good son," she said. "There, the judges are giving out the preserve awards now. They'll start on the pies pretty soon."

The following ten minutes were tense with excitement for Shad and his mother. He knew she was nervous but outwardly she appeared as calm and unconcerned as ever.

They watched the judges begin to cut little wedges

from the pies. Three men were doing the judging—all
local celebrities: the portly manager of the Riverdale
Hotel; the wizened little superintendent of the County
Farm; and Enoch Hanson, a big, pleasant-faced man
who owned the best grocery store in town.

Solemnly they went from pie to pie, sniffing, tasting
and smacking their lips judicially. Shad stole as close
as he dared, but he could tell little of what they were
thinking. Finally they talked together in low voices for
a moment and went back over the double row of pies.

Shad hurried to his mother. "They've cut it down
to three," he whispered, "an' yours is one of 'em.
Look!"

It was impossible to see what was going on now, for
a score of anxious women were crowding closer to the
table. At last the three men put their heads together
and appeared to be nodding in agreement. Enoch
Hanson turned to face the crowd with a smile.

"You've made it mighty tough for us, ladies," he
said. "Best pies we've been called on to taste in five
years. But we've decided the blue ribbon goes to an
apple pie baked by"—he consulted the card in his hand
—"by Mrs. Myron Davis, of Squantic. Myron's a lucky
man!"

Impulsively Shad threw his arms around his mother
and gave her a quick hug. There was a becoming touch
of color in her pale cheeks and a little smile on her
lips when she stepped forward to take the ribbon.

The big grocer bowed gallantly as he handed it to her.

"Wish I could set right down an' finish that pie this minute, Ma'am," he said. "Unfortunately my duties require that I stay hungry till all the rest o' the judging's done."

As soon as awards had been made to the winners in the bread and cake classes, the throng closed in on the tables. It was a tradition of Riverdale Fair that all the food should be eaten when the judging was over. Mrs. Davis managed to get to her pie before anyone else grabbed it, and presently Shad was enjoying a big triangle, luscious with the flavor of green apples, brown sugar, spices and flaky crust.

Before he had finished it, 'Poleon and Hank appeared. Each of them had all he could carry—a slab of pie and a towering wedge of layer cake in either hand.

"Free lunch," mumbled Hank around a mouthful of pie. "Hi, Mrs. Davis. Sure glad you won that blue ribbon. My Ma got a third in the cakes. Only reason she didn't win is that the ol' feller from the County Farm has lost his teeth an' don't like hick'ry nuts."

"How about the boat?" asked Shad. "Did you find it?"

"Yep," 'Poleon replied. "Anyhow, we know where it is. Ol' Joe Banty was here this mornin', bringin' his dahlias to the show. He said it had drifted ashore at his place last night an' he tied it up. We'll get it tonight on our way home."

"Let's stop by the exhibit," said Shad. "I don't know much about flowers, but I sure liked those dahlias he showed us. Anyhow, Joe's such a nice old coot we ought to go in an' give him some encouragement."

The Horticultural Hall was in a wing of the Home Products Building. It was a mass of bright colors and was filled with the heady fragrance of clove pinks and late blooming roses. The dahlias took up one whole side of the big room.

Shad hardly recognized old Joe when he saw him. The ex-clown had stuffed himself into an ancient, greenish-black cutaway coat that failed by half a yard to cover his paunch. He had on a stiff shirt and a clean collar but no necktie. His trousers were held together by a piece of stout string, and he actually had shoes on —old patent-leather shoes with pointed toes that obviously pinched his feet.

It was a warm day and the old fellow was perspiring. He ran a finger around the top of his tight collar and gave the boys a wry smile.

"Durn nuisance, dressin' up," he told them. "Never would ha' made myself this uncomfortable if it wa'n't for the Queen. Look at her. Ain't she a handsome sight?"

The great maroon-and-gold bloom stood in the center of Joe's exhibit, framed by a score of other dahlias, all of varied hues. People passing by stopped and stared at it admiringly.

"There's some big seedsmen here from Boston," Joe whispered to the boys. "One of 'em was here lookin' at it a while back. If the Queen takes a first, there might be a pile o' money in it—mebbe thousan's o' dollars. Wish my boy Sammy could be here to see his ol' man's hour o' triumph."

"When do they do the judging?" Shad asked, a little worried. He knew the dahlia was beautiful but he didn't share the old man's sublime confidence.

"Not till late afternoon, I'm told," Joe replied. "Hope you boys'll be on hand. I got to stay right here an' keep folks from touchin' the Queen."

They wished him luck and returned to the Midway, now teeming with the noonday crowd. There were still half a dozen side shows and amusement places they hadn't investigated, and it was toward one of the latter that Hank steered them. A gaudy cloth sign over the front proclaimed that it was the "Wheel of Fortune."

They could see a big, brightly painted wheel, with numbers on it, and shelves full of prizes that bore corresponding numbers. The barker stood on a chair to look over the heads of the crowd. He tucked a handkerchief around his collar to catch the sweat pouring down his face, lifted his hands and started his spiel.

"Right this way, ladies *and* gennlemen!" he bawled. "A prize fer every number! Everybody wins—nobody loses! Hit the thirteen or the zero an' you get a five

dollar bill!''

The dirty greenbacks between his fingers fluttered temptingly as he waved his arms. "Yessir, ladies *and* gennlemen—I said a five dollar bill! I'm givin' 'em away. On'y a dime a whirl, an' you can't lose. Every-body wins a prize!"

A gawky looking farmer boy of sixteen or seventeen elbowed his way through the crowd and tossed a dime on the counter.

"I'll take a chance," he announced loudly. "Ain't got nothin' to lose, anyhow!" He grinned at the bystanders and they laughed and pushed closer.

"All right," said the barker. "This young feller wants to try the Wheel o' Fortune. Here she goes!"

He gave the wheel a spin and it made a dozen revolutions. Then, moving more and more slowly, it came to a stop. The arrow pointed at the number 13.

"Look a' that!" bellowed the barker. "A thin dime wins this young gennleman a five dollar bill! Here you are, sir, an' don't spend the money on anything foolish!"

'Poleon nudged Shad as the youth backed awkwardly away from the counter holding his precious five dollars.

"Know who that is?" asked the French boy. "It's Elmer Gooch. He pitched for Farmington High last spring. Pretty good lefthander, too. Hi, Elmer!"

The lanky youngster turned, with a startled look on his face. Around him the crowd was pushing eagerly toward the counter. He edged over to 'Poleon's side and grinned sheepishly.

"Hi, Squantic," he said. "You're that fast shortstop that got a three-bagger off me in the Riverdale game an' then stole home."

"That's right," said 'Poleon. "I thought you'd remember. Looks like you're makin' money fast!"

Gooch glanced guiltily at the greasy bill in his hand and shoved it in his pocket. "Don't belong to me," he explained in a low voice. "I'm a shill for this game. Every time the suckers quit bitin', I shove up to the wheel an' lay down a dime. The five bucks I win goes back to Mike, the guy that runs the show."

"Sounds like easy work," said Hank drily. "You get paid for it?"

"Oh, sure—a couple o' bucks a day. But I have to be careful. I look over the crowd an' make sure none of 'em were there before. They might complain to the cops if they saw me win more'n once."

Shad thought it was a pretty shabby way to earn money but he was interested in getting a glimpse of the seamy side of Fair business.

"Do you know a lot of these guys that run the shows?" he asked.

"Yeah, most of 'em," said Gooch. "I shill for a couple of others—the Hoop-la show an' Duke, the Dodger."

"How about this Nellie, the Mermaid, outfit?" Hank inquired.

The boy looked away and shrugged his shoulders. "Never saw 'em before," he answered. "They ain't on the reg'lar circuit. Did you fellers hear about Ki-Ko, the Wild Man?"

"No," said 'Poleon. "I just saw the cage was empty.

Why, what happened?"

"The way I get it, he really was wild," said Gooch. "A big, strong guy but loony in the head. He was all right until some time yesterday afternoon. Then he broke out o' the cage an' just disappeared. The feller that owns the show—name of Maguire—is sort o' worried, I guess. He thinks the wild man might be dangerous, an' it's a cinch the police are goin' to ask him some questions if anything happens."

"Yesterday afternoon, you say he got out," Shad mused. "Any idea what time?"

"Nope. All I heard was they missed him about five-thirty when the crowd started comin' back from the trottin' races. That's when they gener'ly feed him the raw meat.

"Hey, my boss wants me," he muttered. "So long— see you guys around." And resuming his bashful farm-boy attitude, he wandered back toward the "Wheel of Fortune."

Shad looked up at the clock on the Livestock Building. "Gosh," he exclaimed. "It's most race time. I've got to help Yance harness the mare!"

As he sprinted back toward the stables, he passed the deserted Ki-Ko show and saw the empty cage, partly hidden by an old piece of tent canvas. In the back of his mind, a half-formed idea was working. It was the timing of the wild man's disappearance that stuck in his memory. It must have happened around five

o'clock—a little after or a little before. He wanted to
stop and find out more facts, but the minutes were
passing and he knew Yance wouldn't like it if he stayed
away any longer. Later, when he had more time to
think, he would try to make the whole thing add up.

The trainer was inside Sequoia's box stall when Shad
arrived, out of breath. He didn't look up from what
he was doing. The boy saw that he was wrapping a
spiral bandage with care around the mare's left foreleg.

"Anything wrong with her, Yance?" he asked anx-
iously.

The gypsy didn't smile as he glanced up. "Can't be
sure yet," he said. "She looked all right when you
brought her in this morning, but since then I noticed

she seemed to favor that left foot a little. Checked the shoe an' there's nothing wrong there. I'm hoping it's just a mite o' stiffness in a muscle, an' it'll be gone as soon as she warms up. Run out the sulky an' get the harness ready. Our race is due to start at two o'clock."

They had the mare harnessed before the first call of "Drivers up" came over the loud-speaker. Shad held her bridle while Yance slipped into his moleskins and blue sateen shirt, donned driving cap and goggles and pulled on his gloves. Then he settled himself on the seat, with the mare's long silky tail anchored under him.

"All right, lady," the gypsy said softly. "Time to be a-moving."

Shad stood aside and watched them go. It made him wince to see Sequoia limp a little as she took the first few steps. But her eyes were bright and her ears pricked forward eagerly. All she asked was a chance to trot.

NINE

BEFORE Yance and the mare reached the track gate, Shad saw them stop for a moment. Mr. Martin was talking to the trainer. He went forward to stroke Sequoia's neck, leaned down and ran his hand over her left foreleg, then nodded to Yance. As the sulky rolled out on the track, he returned to the stand.

A moment later young Bud Martin came back to the stable.

"Hi, Shad," he grinned. "What's up—something happen to Sequoia? I see Yance has her bandaged."

"She acts kind of lame," Shad replied unhappily. "I can't figure what the trouble is—unless I handled her wrong this morning. Yance let me work her an' she went as smooth as silk."

Bud shaded his eyes and looked toward the upper turn where the horses were warming up. "She's trotting all right now," he said. "Want to go over an' watch the race?"

"I've got to stay here," Shad told him. "There've been some queer things going on, an' I know Yance wouldn't want me to leave the horses alone—even with Tug on the job."

"What sort o' queer things do you mean?" asked Bud.

"Nothing you can really put a finger on. There was somebody sneaking around the stable last night around five o'clock. I didn't catch sight of him, but I think he ducked out through a hole in the high fence. Then I spotted a guy clocking Cedar's Boy, an' he looked to me like that big lug in the green shirt we figured was in the bookie gang. Probably it doesn't mean a thing, but I feel better when there's somebody here with the horses."

"Look," said Bud generously, "I'm not as keen on this race business as you are. I'll stay here an' you go ahead over to the track. Tell me about it when you get back."

Shad needed no second invitation. He thanked Bud and made for the track at top speed.

When he squeezed his way through the crowd to the rail, the starter had already scored the field once and was bringing them down for a second try. Sequoia was in number three position, and Yance had her nicely lined up with the pole horse, a long-legged chestnut by the name of Kangaroo.

"Watch it there, Nichols!" blared the starter's voice.

"Number Six! Hold your horse in! That's better—that's— GO!"

Shad had been holding his breath. Now he let it out in a yell. "Yea, Sequoia! Go it, girl! Get that pole!"

She was trying, as he could see, with all her gallant heart. But the long-striding Kangaroo had put on a burst of early speed that she couldn't overcome. As they rounded into the backstretch she was in second place, her head even with the pole horse's sulky wheels, and the rest of the field trailed out behind.

Their positions remained unchanged as they came down the stretch and went into the second lap. Yance looked calm enough as his face flashed past. He was driving a steady race, holding something in reserve. The other horses were out of it now. This heat was between Sequoia and Kangaroo and the crowd howled approval as they came to the head of the final straightaway.

Shad saw Kangaroo's driver bring the whip down hard. The big horse responded by pulling out to a full-length lead, then overdid his rush. He broke momen-

tarily. It was only two or three seconds till he was trotting again, but that was all the mare needed. Flattened
out and going like the wind, she went under the wire
a winner by a stride.

Her limp was hardly noticeable when she came off
the track. Yance jumped down from the sulky as Shad
took her head. He felt of the twitching muscles in the
mare's shoulder and leg and wasn't wholly satisfied.

"Bring her blanket," he told the boy. "I'll keep her
walking. She did all right, that heat, but I'm afraid of
letting her get stiff."

Sequoia's tawny coat was rumpled by patches of
dried sweat when Shad took the blanket off her. Her
step wasn't quite as eager as it had been, but she cocked
her ears and lifted her head for the checkrein to be
fastened.

Yance patted her cheek. "It's got to be this time, old
girl," he told her lovingly. "You couldn't stand a third
heat, an' I wouldn't ask you to try."

Getting the field off the second time was a slow and
difficult business. After they had scored raggedly on

three tries, the starter's voice was edgy and the drivers' tempers hot. The fourth time they came down there was some semblance of a line, and they got a belated go signal.

Yance had the pole with Sequoia by virtue of winning the first heat. He took the mare off to a fast start and Kangaroo failed to pass her with his opening rush. After that, the race was a repetition of the first heat, except that this time Sequoia was on the rail and holding the lead. On the last turn Kangaroo made his move. His driver had learned a lesson now. He brought the big horse up without a break and they were trotting head-and-head at the top of the stretch.

Shad took a deep breath and held it. His fists were tightly clenched and his heart beat as fast as Sequoia's pounding hoofs.

"Keep on, gal," he whispeerd. "Keep coming!"

The mare's ears were back, her head level with her body, and she was putting all she had into that punishing drive. Yance held the whip ready but he never used it. No lashing could have brought a greater effort from Sequoia than she was already giving.

Both horses kept up the killing pace right to the finish, but it was the sorrel mare's nose that flashed first under the wire.

The spectators packed in the stands yelled themselves hoarse at that victory. Shad's throat was too dry to shout, and his eyes were scared as he watched the horses slow down and turn. There was no question about the game little mare's lameness now. She was almost hobbling on three legs.

The boy stood miserably by the gate and waited for Yance to bring her out. The gypsy had dismounted from the sulky and was leading her gently by the bridle. His lean face looked bleak and drawn. Over the public address system a sing-song voice announced the result of the race.

"The two-twenty trot—won by Mr. Martin's Sequoia in straight heats. Time, two-fourteen and two-seventeen."

Shad wasn't listening. He took the mare's other rein and walked slowly, keeping pace with Yance. Sequoia's checkrein had been loosened and her tired head hung down. Their advance toward the stable was like a funeral march.

Hartley Martin and Bud joined them as they started to take the harness off.

"I never saw a gamer race," said the dairyman with a choke in his voice. "Nice piece of driving, Yance. I called the vet from the phone-booth under the stand. He'll be here in an hour."

Shad undid the last buckle and carried the harness into the tack room. He was glad to get out of sight for there were tears in his eyes. He didn't know how serious the mare's injury might be, but he had a gnawing fear that he was to blame for it. In his ignorance it was possible he had handled her wrong that morning.

Yance was talking when he returned to the little group around Sequoia. "She's got too much heart," said the gypsy. "I couldn't've held her down if I'd tried. She meant to win that one."

"Well," Mr. Martin answered. "Nobody's to blame unless it's myself for letting her race. I'd gladly give that five hundred dollar purse to know she'll be fit to trot again."

They rubbed her down with care and Shad brought fresh straw for her bed. She was lying down when Doc Royall, the veterinary, arrived. His dusty little coupé came bouncing in over the turf and stopped in front of the stable with a squeal of brakes.

"I came as quick as I could, Bud," he told Hartley Martin. "Hate to see anything wrong with that mare o' yours. I helped bring her into the world an' I'm pretty fond of her."

He went into the loose-box and the rest of them waited in silence outside.

"Come on, girl," they could hear him saying. "I know it hurts, but you've got to stand up or I can't do much for you. H'm—pretty painful, eh? All right, take it easy while I see what I can find."

It was a full half hour before he came out, wiping the perspiration from his forehead with a blue bandanna. They looked at him with mingled hope and fear, but he took his own time about speaking.

"It's not too bad," he said, at last. "Nothing that can't be cured, with patience. I was afraid of a bowed tendon but I reckon it's only a badly pulled muscle. If she hadn't gone that second heat she'd probably have been well in a week. The way it is you'll be lucky if she trots again before July. I'd get her back to the farm an' put her in her own stall with plenty of soft bedding. If she begins to feel better this fall, let her out in the paddock when the weather's warm. Medicine won't help much. It's just a matter of time an' her own good constitution."

Mr. Martin thanked the vet and paid him. "That all sounds good to me," he said. "I was afraid she'd never go sound again. I'm not so anxious to race her but I'm counting on her for a brood mare."

"Fine!" the doctor beamed. "Let me know when you plan to breed her. With the right sire she'll give you a foal that'll make the whole harness world sit up an' take notice! I reckon there never was a gamer mare since Goldsmith Maid."

Bud gave a sigh of relief when the veterinary drove away. "Gosh!" he exclaimed. "I feel better!"

"Me, too," echoed Shad from the bottom of his heart. "I didn't know—I thought maybe she'd have to be—destroyed!"

"Dad wouldn't have done that, if there was any way to save her," the other boy laughed. "But I could see you were worried."

Bud and his father went back to the stands, but Shad
didn't feel like watching any more racing that afternoon. He carried water for the horses, washed and
oiled Sequoia's harness and asked Yance if there were
any more chores he wanted done.

"Guess not," said the gypsy. "You can take a couple
of hours off if you want. Be back at suppertime?"

The boy replied that he would. "Old Joe Banty's
showing his dahlias," he explained. "We sort o' promised we'd be there for the judging."

Hank and 'Poleon were nowhere in sight when he
entered the Horticultural Hall. A good-sized crowd of
women and a fair scattering of men were present, however. The three judges were already working on one
side of the exhibit. Shad made his way over to the
dahlia section and had no difficulty in finding old Joe.

The fat man's face was almost purple and he mopped
away streams of sweat with a handkerchief. His collar
had long since wilted to a rag.

"I ain't had on so many clothes in summertime for
twenty years," he mumbled in Shad's ear. "An' these
durn shoes! They're killin' me. Had 'em off for a spell,
but with all these ladies hangin' 'round, I figgered I
had to put 'em on again."

"Joe," said Shad, "I've been wondering about that
boat of ours. You didn't see anybody around, did you—
I mean someone that might have swiped it from where
it was tied up, back o' the Fair Grounds?"

For an instant there was a scared look in the old man's eyes. Then he turned his head hastily away.

"Why, no," he said, as if in surprise. "Didn't see a soul. Like I told the boys, the boat must ha' broke loose an' drifted down. It was stuck in the mud there under the bank, right below my landin'. Say, those judges are 'bout ready to come over this way, it looks like. That feller back of 'em, in the gray suit an' panama hat— he's Mr. Gardner, the seedsman. Stopped by a while back an' asked me about the Queen. He's interested, all right."

Shad recognized only one of the judges—the florist who had a shop on Central Square. He was a fussy little man in a frock coat that looked like an undertaker's, and his thin, brown hair was combed carefully over his bald spot.

"Now, in the dahlias," they could hear him telling his associates above the murmur of the crowd, "I think you'll find these of Mrs. Brewster's are outstanding."

Another judge—a big, slow-moving, white-haired man—smiled. "Suppose we just look at all of 'em, Ferd," he said mildly. "Then we can make up our own minds."

There were a few snickers among the bystanders, and the red-faced florist had no more to say. Methodically the judges moved down the line of flowers. Each one made notes on a little pad as he examined the blooms.

Shad thought old Joe would burst before they reached his exhibit. He was so shaky he could hardly get the handkerchief out of his pocket to wipe his moist, red face. But when the group finally approached, the old fellow squared his plump shoulders and greeted them with a courtly bow.

The big, white-haired judge gave him a nod and a smile in return, then began, unhurriedly, to study the blossoms. He felt of the stems and leaves, tilted each flower to view it from several angles, and jotted down his findings on the pad he carried. When he came to the Caterwaul Queen he looked baffled for a moment. Then he stooped to read the name on the wooden tag and turned to scrutinize old Joe with fresh interest.

"New variety," he remarked. "You developed it yourself, Mr. Banty?"

"That's right," said the old fellow, beaming. "Been tryin' a long time, but I got her at last."

The judge nodded. He examined the bloom more carefully and wrote several lines in his notes. The others evidently respected his opinion, for they, too, gave the big maroon-and-gold flower special attention.

It took half an hour for the trio to complete their judging. Then, for ten minutes more, they stood in a huddle, deciding on the awards. At last Shad saw the big man with the white hair pick up a number of colored ribbons from the table. He held up his hand for silence and the chatter in the hall subsided.

"Folks," he said, in a voice everyone could hear, "you've got a mighty fine collection of flowers. The judges want to congratulate every exhibitor here. We've had to make our decisions on merit an' it wasn't easy. I'll read out the awards."

He cleared his throat and looked at the paper in his hand.

"Best exhibit in the show," he read, "Mr. Joseph Banty, of Riverdale."

There was a gasp of surprise, then applause.

"Best in the dahlia class," he went on, "Mr. Joseph

Banty."

"Best single bloom of any kind, Mr. Banty's new dahlia, the 'Caterwaul Queen'!"

In the roar of cheers that went up, nobody heard the thud of a body hitting the floor. Shad, turning to congratulate his old friend, found Joe lying flat on his back.

Scared, the boy dropped to his knees. He was loosening the fat man's collar when Joe sputtered, opened his eyes and tried to sit up.

"Take it easy," Shad pleaded. "Just lie still, Joe, till I can find a doctor."

"Doctor!" the old fellow wheezed. "I ain't been sick in forty years! All I want is for you to tell me if I heard right."

"Yes, Joe," said the boy. "You heard right. You won first in just about everything in the show!"

TEN

OLD Joe was hardly back on his feet when Mr. Gardner, the Boston seedsman, came pushing through the crowd of well-wishers.

"Well, Mr. Banty," he said, shaking the fat man's hand, "I think we can do business with that new dahlia of yours."

"Wouldn't be surprised," Joe answered drily. "What sort of a proposition you makin'?"

Mr. Gardner hemmed and hawed a little. "Of course," he said, "any new flower has to prove itself. It may take several years before we know it breeds true. We're prepared to offer you fifty dollars for the root, and a percentage on sales—"

"Listen," Joe Banty interrupted scornfully. "The Queen'll breed true. What you think I been doin', the last eight years? Besides, I'm an old man. I ain't interested in waitin' for a percentage. You want to pay me a thousan' dollars cash? If you ain't interested I can find folks that are. I know what that dahlia's worth."

The city man seemed a trifle disconcerted. "Now, now, Mr. Banty," he said, "let's not be hasty. A cash settlement might be arranged, of course. If you'll let me take this blossom back to Boston and talk it over with our firm, I'll let you know in a couple of days."

Old Joe nodded. "That makes more sense," he agreed. "I'll be lookin' for an answer by Friday, an' if I don't hear from you then, I'll find a buyer somewhere else. There's more Queen blooms at home about as good as this one."

He gave Mr. Gardner his address and placed the huge dahlia carefully in a cardboard box. When the seedsman was gone, Joe leaned against the display shelf and Shad saw that all his bluster had left him. He looked pale and his hands trembled.

"That was mostly bluff," he whispered. "Fact is I got to have the money."

"Why, Joe?" the boy asked. "You mean you're in some kind o' trouble?"

"Not me." The old man seemed to realize he had said more than he intended. He pulled himself together with an effort. "Forget it, son," he mumbled, and turned away to rearrange his flowers.

Shad wished he could help him but he didn't know how. Working his way out through the throng, he was starting back toward the stables when he ran into Hank Wetherbee.

"Did you hear the latest about Ki-Ko, the Wild Man?" asked Hank.

"Only what we heard this noon—that he'd broken out an' disappeared. Why—what else?"

"Seems a farmer a little ways south o' town heard his chickens cacklin' early this mornin', an' looked out toward the henhouse. 'Twasn't light enough to see much, but he claims there was a man covered with red hair sneakin' away from there. He took his gun out an' shot at the hairy guy an' thinks he hit him. They found some blood in the grass afterward, but the feller got away. The sheriff's sent a posse out lookin' for him, an' they're pretty sure it's Ki-Ko. Say, I didn't get to the flower show. How'd ol' Joe make out?"

Shad was thinking hard. "What?" he asked vaguely. "Oh—he did fine. Took most o' the prizes, an' I guess he'll sell the new dahlia for plenty o' money."

"Well," said the other boy, "I've got to find 'Poleon an' head for home. See you tomorrow."

Shad returned to the stable, hardly noticing where he was going. His mind was busy fitting together the pieces of the puzzle that had bothered him earlier that day. It was coming clearer every moment. He thought he knew, now, who the "Wild Man" was—and why old Joe Banty needed cash. That half-witted son of his, who had disappeared years ago, was probably hidden somewhere around the cabin by the river, nursing a shotgun wound. He hoped Hank and 'Poleon wouldn't run across him when they stopped to get the boat. He might be crazy and dangerous, but that didn't make Shad less sorry for his father.

Yance got up from the feedbox where he had been sitting, sucking on his pipe.

"Now you're back," he told the boy, "I'd better go eat. Then you can get your supper."

Shad looked into Sequoia's stall and found it lonesomely empty. They must have taken the mare back to Red Horse Hill in the truck. He was going to miss her.

He sat down on the feedbox and called Tug to keep him company. The big white dog lay quietly at his feet while Shad wrestled with a real problem. Probably he ought to go to the police or the sheriff or somebody and tell them where they might find their "Wild Man." But after all, he didn't know for sure. It was just a guess. And his sympathies were all with old Joe, doing his best to keep his feeble-minded son out of trouble.

He was still trying to make up his mind when Yance returned and sent him over to the boardinghouse. Most of the horsemen had already left, but a few grooms and drivers still sat at one of the long tables.

Shad listened to their talk while he ate roast pork and applesauce. At first the conversation was about horses—the afternoon's races—how this or that favorite was training. Then he heard a swipe at the other end of the table mention the "Wild Man."

"A feller I know was out with the posse all day," he said. "They had five cars an' covered most o' the county. Never found hide nor hair of him. Reckon they won't, either. I bet he's clear up in the hills by now—up in the woods beyond Blue Job."

"Or else dead," another put in. "Remember, he was shot pretty bad. They'll probably find his bones under a bush somewhere, come spring."

"Poor guy!" said the first groom. "They say he was harmless—just a big, dumb nitwit. Maguire treated him all right. Gave him his grub an' a little money to spend. There was no lock on the cage. He could ha' walked out like he usually did between shows. Only this time he got a crazy notion an' busted the bars. Can you beat that?"

The boy was still eating his dessert when they went out. But their talk had helped him make up his mind. Whether the hairy man was Sam Banty or not, Shad figured it wasn't his business to load any more trouble on him.

It was dark and quiet back at the stable. Yance rose and stretched when the boy appeared.

"Think I'll go into town a little while," he said. "I'll see what news I can pick up around the hotel. There'll be some more entries in for the Free-for-All by now. You can turn in if you want. Tomorrow's the colt's big day, an' you'll be giving him his morning exercise."

Shad was tired. When he had made sure that Cedar's
Boy and Redwood were comfortably bedded, he snug-
gled down in the clean straw and went to sleep almost
at once.

.   .   .

"Roll out, there!" came Yance's cheery voice. "Rise
an' shine! Sun's most up an' there's horses to work."

Shad rubbed the sleep out of his eyes and ran to
wash. It was going to be another hot, fair day—good
racing weather. When he led Redwood out of his stall
the colt fairly danced with energy and high spirits.

"He's feeling right," said Yance approvingly. "Now
the trick is to let him limber up without losing that
edge. I'd say about five laps, jogging, would be enough.
But he won't be happy unless you let him out a little
on the last one—maybe half a lap."

Already the boy felt more at home in the training
cart. He didn't have the stop watch with him this time,
and it was just as well, for he found the colt all he
wanted to handle. It was still before sunrise when
they pranced out on the track, and only one or two
other horses were there before them.

Redwood wanted to go, and at the end of the first
lap the boy's arms ached from holding him down.
After that he seemed content to jog along smoothly.
Shad counted off the laps, and as they rounded into
the backstretch on the fifth time around he lifted the

reins a little.

That was all the encouragement the colt asked. His slim chestnut barrel settled lower in the shafts and his legs began to fly as he almost snatched the seat out from under Shad.

"Easy there, boy," the young driver told him. "Keep it smooth. You've got a race today, so save some o' that stuff."

He steadied the colt's speed, took him wide around the turn to give another sulky plenty of room, then edged in again toward the pole and came down to the wire eased off.

"Nice driving," Yance told him when they returned to the stable. "I was watching all the way, an' you've got a good pair o' hands. Cool him out an' rub him down now, while I see how the big horse goes."

They unharnessed Redwood and put the blanket on him. As Yance climbed up behind Cedar's Boy, Shad remembered something.

"Wonder if that clocker's likely to be out again," he said. "If you see a short, husky guy in a green sport shirt, that's the one."

"I'll be watching," Yance nodded. "Keep that colt moving till he's dry."

Shad was currying Redwood in his stall when the trainer brought the big bay in.

There was a grim look around Yance's mouth and his brows were wrinkled in a frown. Shad waited for him to speak, but he kept silent until Cedar's Boy was unharnessed.

"I don't like it," he said at last.

"You mean you saw the fellow in the green shirt?"

"Yes, he was there. Sort of sneaked up to the fence while I was finishing the warm-up laps. He was your man all right. But when he left there was another guy, that met him, up near the far turn."

"What did he look like?" asked Shad.

"That's the trouble. I didn't see his face. But he walked like somebody I used to know. He's on the small side—short an' thin—coal-black hair. The hair's wrong. The man I knew would be over sixty now. Except for that I'd have thought it was the same fellow."

Shad was excited. "I know the man!" he exclaimed. "Sure—he was in the Mermaid tent along with the others. An' we noticed his black hair. His face looked old an' white. Maybe he's got some kind o' dye on his hair!"

Yance straightened up and stared at him. "His face— you say it looked white? That might be it. A lot of years in prison would do that. An' hair dye! By golly, Shad, I believe it *was* the guy I knew. I believe it was Harko Dan—the horse-thief!"

"That's the one that stole old Cedar!" Shad exclaimed. "Bud told me—way back when Mr. Martin was a kid!"

Yance nodded. "I could be wrong," he said soberly.

"I sure hope I am. Harko Dan hasn't any love for me or the Martin family. It's bad news to have him around."

Shad did some thinking while he finished brushing down the colt. "Look," he suggested to Yance. "The papers said this Harko Dan broke out o' jail, an' there's

a reward out for him. Why don't you go see Chief Rooney, soon as you've had breakfast. I'd say the chances are mighty good that he'll find the man he's after in the back o' that side show."

"I'll do that," said the gypsy. "I don't like to leave the horses alone, even for a few minutes. So if you can wait to eat, I'll run over to the boardinghouse now. Don't let anybody come near those stalls. Tug'll be here to help."

Two hours went by before the trainer returned. Shad was too excited to realize he was hungry. He finished currying the bay horse, washed and oiled the harness and sat down to wait.

Finally, a little after eight o'clock, he saw Yance coming across the open ground at the end of the track. The gypsy's face was glum.

"Everything all right here?" he asked as he reached the stable.

"Yes," said Shad. "What happened? Did you catch him?"

Yance shook his head. "The chief got two men an' surrounded that Mermaid place," he said. "There wasn't a soul there except the owner—a rat-faced guy by the name of Morse. He was asleep in the back o' the tent. No books, no record of any bets. Made me look a little foolish. But the worst of it is, they know the police are on to 'em now, an' they'll hole up somewhere else."

Shad was more than disappointed. He saw now what a bad mistake he had made. If the raid had been held off until later in the day, when the bookie ring was at work, everything might have been fine. Now the gypsy horse-thief—if it was he—would be twice as hard to catch.

It was late in the forenoon when Mr. Martin and Bud drove up. The boy was fairly bursting with pride.

"You should have been over at the Livestock Building this morning," he told Shad. "They judged the dairy cattle an' our Mountain Majesty took another blue ribbon—champion Guernsey in the show! One of his daughters placed second in the heifer class, too.

Now if Redwood comes through in the Futurity it'll be quite a day for the Mason & Martin Farm. How's the colt look?"

"He's ready," said Shad. "Full o' ginger, but Yance'll keep him in line."

Bud eyed him wonderingly. "Say—what's the trou-

ble?" he asked. "You look sort of down-in-the-mouth."

Before Shad had time to reply, Mr. Martin beckoned to him.

"Yance has been telling me about this character he saw this morning," he said. "I understand you got a good look at him the other day. Could you describe him?"

"Sure," Shad answered. "He's on the small side. About five-foot-six—weighs maybe a hundred an' thirty. His hair's a dead black color. Eyes dark. Face thin an' wrinkled like an old man's. An' skin so pale one o' the boys said he looked like a ghost. You saw him, Bud. Isn't that about right?"

"That's the way I'd describe him," said Bud. "Why

—who is he?"

"It was the way he walked," Yance put in. "You remember that walk—short, springy steps, like a cat,
sort of?"

Hartley Martin nodded and his face was grave. "I
think you're right," he said. "Sounds like Harko Dan
to me. I'm going over an' call up the farm. It won't
hurt to have the hired men on watch. Because, if I
know that fellow, he's the kind that would hold a
grudge a long time."

ELEVEN

THE Futurity, open to two-year-old trotters and pacers, was scheduled for four o'clock—the next to the last race of the day.

Redwood had eaten a good breakfast and a light feed at noon. Thoroughly rested, he was as fit as a youngster could be for the test of speed ahead. Unlike the older horses he hadn't sensed the coming race, and he seemed surprised and pleased when Shad put the harness on him.

Yance buckled him into the shafts carefully. It was the same sulky that Sequoia had pulled the day before and the colt was about her size. The shadow roll was adjusted on his nose and the checkrein hooked up.

When the call came and they started for the gate, the Martins were there to see them off. Mr. Martin looked the young chestnut over critically and grinned at Yance.

"Looks like a chip off the old block," he said. "Cedar

was just his age when Uncle John and I started training him. Best luck I can wish you is to hope Redwood's just as fast as his granddad!"

Yance nodded, touched his whip to the visor of his cap and guided the eager colt out on the track.

"I'll stay with Cedar's Boy," Bud volunteered. "You go ahead an' watch, Shad. We can trade off after the first heat."

Shad shook his head. "You go along with your dad," he said. "I'll look out for the horse now—Tug and I."

He could see the upper turn from his seat in front of the stable, and a little of the stretch. Nearly a dozen colts and fillies were on the track now. They were skittish, nervous, hard to handle. He could hear the voice of the starter over the amplifier—impatient at first, then sarcastic.

"*Mister* White! will you get that colt turned around? We've got to get a race started here, and we like all the horses to go the same way o' the track! . . . All right, now, Mr. Mosher, this isn't a running race. Does your filly know how to trot? If so, let's see her do it."

They scored again and again. Even from that distance Shad could see that most of them were chafing and sweating. Redwood looked about as steady as any colt in the field, but he was beginning to fidget. At last they went down fairly well bunched and no bell clanged. They were off!

The boy got to his feet and waited thirty seconds—

forty seconds—staring at the empty end of the track. He could hear the low rumble of the crowd, mounting, growing hoarser. Then, far across the oval, the heads and backs of tiny horses and their drivers appeared past the end of the grandstand. Shad did his best to make out the colors but all he could see was that the driver on the lead sulky wore red and white. Where was Yance's blue blouse? Where was Redwood?

He saw them when they swept around the turn—the young chestnut on the outside, two lengths back but coming strong. There were at least three horses ahead of him. Yance didn't seem to be pushing the colt. After all there was another lap to go.

They vanished behind the stand and once more Shad had the ordeal of waiting. He climbed up on the feed-box and stood on tiptoe so that he could get a better view. It was pure torture to hear the frenzied cheering of the spectators and not know what was happening.

At last they came in sight again. With a thrill he saw that Redwood had pulled up to second place, his eager head alongside the wheel of the leading sulky. The driver in the red and white silks was using his whip as they rounded into the final stretch, and his lanky brown trotter was going like a steam engine. But the chestnut colt was still gaining when the grand-stand hid them from view.

Shad got slowly down from the box. "Gosh, Tug," he sighed, "I don't know if I can stand it till I know who won."

He walked up and down, biting his nails, for nearly a minute. Then the hoped-for announcement came over the loudspeaker:

"Winner of the first heat—Number Four, Redwood, owned by Hartley Martin. Time, two-twelve-and-a-half."

The colts and fillies came off the track and Shad raced out to take Redwood's bridle as Yance stepped down from the sulky.

"That must have been close!" the boy exclaimed. "The brown horse was still ahead, the last I saw."

"Yep," said Yance. "We had to hustle. That was Milestone Hanover, with Bill Drake up. Redwood didn't take him till the last fifty yards."

While they were walking the blanketed colt up and down, Bud came running over from the stand.

"Great stuff, Yance!" he cried. "Dad says that was nice driving. An' Redwood's got plenty left, hasn't he?"

"Enough, I guess," said the trainer. "You can't always tell about a two-year-old. An' that Hanover colt is tough competition. Some o' the others, too. It's a good field."

When the second heat was called, Bud insisted on taking Shad's place at the stable. "You get out there an' pull for the colt," he grinned. "Be sure you bring him home in front."

Shad accompanied Yance and Redwood as far as the

gate, then found a place along the rail where he had
a full view of the half-mile oval.

The field of juveniles came straggling back on the
track and the starter warned them sharply. "Let's cut
out the fooling this time," he barked. "You've had
your fun. Now try a good, clean start."

They were turning near the head of the stretch.
There was a moment of confusion and then they came
down, fairly well bunched, with Redwood pacing easily
on the pole.

To the amazement of everyone, including the drivers, there was no scoring bell. "Go!" yelled the starter,
and the heat was on.

Shad gave a gasp of dismay, for Yance had held the
colt back expecting the recall signal. As they crossed
the line a slim little bay filly flashed into the lead and
stole the pole position! At the same time Milestone
Hanover had gone up on the outside, and Redwood
was boxed on the first turn.

Shad watched, breathless, as they straightened into
the backstretch. Drake, driving the brown colt, was
making no effort to overtake the flying filly. He respected Redwood's speed and it was obvious that he
meant to keep his rival bottled up.

Twice Yance tried to pull the colt back and get out
of the squeeze, but the rest of the field was crowding
too close. Shad groaned. At the end of the first lap
they were still in the same position—the bay filly lead-

ing on the pole, Redwood right behind her, and the Hanover colt lapping them on the outside.

"Time of the half—one-nine," intoned the loud-speaker.

That was slow—too slow. There were good young-sters in the field and something was bound to happen soon. On the lower turn it came. A red roan colt that had been pacing fourth started his rush. As they swung into the far stretch he nosed up to pass Milestone Han-over, and Drake, startled, let the brown colt out. That was the moment Yance had been waiting for. Even at that distance Shad saw him pull the young chestnut out to the right, his reaching forefeet close behind Drake's sulky wheels.

The bay filly put on a gallant spurt of her own, and as they rounded into the last curve the four were so closely bunched it looked like anybody's race.

Shad gripped the rail so hard his knuckles went white. Under his breath he was urging Redwood on—pulling him down the track with all his will power.

The roan colt, tearing along on the outside, broke under the terrific pressure. He went into the air in an awkward gallop, his snapped hopples flying. And into the gap he left, Redwood moved like a tawny streak.

They were in the last stretch now—the three of them almost abreast. On the pole the little filly trotted gamely, her flying legs a blur. The big, long-reaching Hanover colt was in the middle, a nose ahead. And flanking him came Redwood, his rocking, sidewheel gait quickening with every stride.

The roar of the crowd was almost deafening. This was a horse race—as close a finish as any fan could ask!

As they flashed past the boy at the rail he screamed Redwood's name, but his voice was lost in the tumult. He strained out as far as he could reach to see what happened in that last rush to the wire. But from where he stood it was impossible to tell the winner.

"Dead heat!" someone beside him shouted above the subsiding clamor. "If it ain't, it's sure a photo-finish."

The big field swung into the curve, slowed down, and turned raggedly, jogging back toward the post. There was no announcement. The seconds ticked away into minutes and excitement mounted again in the stands. Cries of "Who won?" came from the crowd. And the sweating horses milled up and down in confusion in front of the judges' stand.

At last the voice on the loud-speaker broke silence. "Sorry to keep you waiting, folks," it bellowed. "We had to get the official photos and they're coming up now. The winner—" there was a dramatic pause—"is Number Four, Redwood, by a head!"

Shad let out a whoop and jumped into the air while a volley of cheers rose from the grandstand. The announcer waited till they quieted a little before he gave the time of the heat—two-thirteen-and-a-quarter.

Yance drove out through the gate and Hartley Martin was there to greet him. "Well," he told the driver, beaming, "we know we've got a good one now. Did you know you went the last half at close to a two-eight clip? That's sure traveling for a youngster like Redwood!"

Shad was happy as he helped take the colt's harness off and cooled him out. He was really a part of the team. He had helped condition a winner and was tremendously proud of the result.

Old Billy Randall strolled over to join the group by the stable. His face was crinkled in a smile of triumph.

"I knew it," he said. "Remember what I told ye, the day that colt was foaled? He's Cedar all over again, I said. An' durned if he ain't. Never seen a baby pace

any faster or show any more heart in a stretch drive. Bring him along easy an' he'll give ye a two-two or two-three record a couple o' years from now."

"What's the news, Billy?" Mr. Martin asked. "Any fresh entries for the Free-for-All?"

"Plenty," the old trainer nodded. "You're goin' to have yer hands full, Yance. I reckon Bud—Bud, senior, I mean—ain't forgot a blue roan mare named Chocorua that Sam Felton used to own. She could trot like blazes. Mighty near took ol' Cedar on the snow-path once."

"You bet I remember her!" Hartley Martin replied with feeling. "I hated her, too. Had a head like a snake. But, boy—how she could move!"

"Well," said Randall, "they just unloaded a mare from the van that's a dead ringer for her. I snooped around a little an' found out she belongs to Win Felton—that's ol' Sam's spoiled son. You know him, too, Bud. He was a pasty-faced kid a little older'n you. Moved down to Boston after he finished college, an' he's got a nice string o' trotters. This one's called Chan somethin'—Chansonette, I guess—but Chocorua was her third dam, an' the blood shows strong."

"What's her record?" Yance put in.

"Nobody seems to know," said the old man. "Funny, too, because she's raced plenty on the western tracks. One feller tol' me he'd heard she could go in two-five, an' I wouldn't wonder if that was about right."

Young Bud whistled. "Sounds like Grand Circuit

time," he said. "Are there any more that good?"

"Could be," Billy Randall drawled. "I know of two hosses that come here straight off the Grand. One's a four-year-old stallion named Jester. Big black feller by His Majesty. Abbedale blood, an' that means he can pace. The other's a homely, long-legged gray hoss from

Ohio. If I'd never seen Greyhound trot I wouldn't have noticed him special. But this one looks like he could be Greyhound's son—if he had any sons."

Hartley Martin grinned. "Ought to be quite a race," he said. "An' don't forget that Mischief Direct mare from Maine. They tell me she's plenty fast, an' she'll be handled by Ken Wicks. He's about as good a driver as they come. Wouldn't you say so, Yance?"

The gypsy nodded. "There'll be a lot o' good drivers in this one," he said. "An' good horses, too. But we'll be in there trying."

Young Bud came into the stall where Shad was currying the colt. "You going to watch the pulling contest tomorrow?" he asked.

"I might, if Yance doesn't need me. What time does it come off?"

"About ten in the morning. Thought you might like to see it because there's an entry from Squantic Mill."

"Big Babe?" asked Shad, with interest. "Gee, I wouldn't miss that. She's one o' the sights o' the town. Ever see her?"

"No," the other boy said. "You mean just *one* horse? This contest is for work teams."

"All right, Babe's a work team all by herself. You wait an' see. If Yance lets me off I'll meet you over there at ten."

Bud and his father left for home a few minutes later.

"Mind you keep a good watch on the horses," Hartley Martin cautioned them as he got into the car. "I know you won't leave 'em alone, even for a minute. I'll talk to the chief of police again on the way out."

At Yance's suggestion, Shad went to supper early. The gypsy and Billy Randall were still sitting in front of the stable smoking and talking when he returned at dusk. They continued their conversation a while, then strolled off in the direction of the boardinghouse, and he was on his own.

An hour passed. The night shut down, dark and sultry, and Shad watched the lights go out, one by one, in the long line of stables. Still Yance didn't come back. Probably he and the old trainer had run across some cronies among the horsemen and were swapping yarns. The boy yawned a few times, realized how sleepy he was and debated going to bed. After all, he knew Tug would wake him if anything was wrong.

He finally compromised with his conscience by spreading an armful of straw in front of Cedar's Boy's stall and curling up there. He could see a star or two in the black sky beyond the overhanging eaves. With another deep yawn he rolled on his side and fell into an uneasy half-doze.

TWELVE

IF he had been really asleep, Shad would probably not have heard the noise. As it was, the thing that woke him was a sudden movement by the white dog lying at his side.

Tug was up, a low growl rumbling in his throat. In an instant the boy, too, was on his feet. It was too dark for him to see anything but he could hear the muffled thud of running feet off to his left. He took a step or two in that direction, then remembered the flashlight that hung on a nail in the tack shed. Hurrying back, he groped for the flash and found it. In the dim circle of light it threw he saw a broken pitchfork handle which he picked up as a possible weapon. Then he ran after Tug.

The unmown hay stood knee-high along the fence beyond the stable, and the flashlight showed him a faint track where feet had beaten down the grass. He had gone less than a hundred yards when he saw a white blur in the dark ahead. As he ran nearer he made out the figure of the bull terrier and a darker shape on the ground. The dog was growling steadily. Now he heard another sound—a half-gasp, half-moan of terror.

At first, Shad couldn't see the man's face, for he lay on his stomach, hands outstretched. Then, as the light fell around him he moved his head. A bushy white beard came into view. The lips moved jerkily and a hoarse voice issued from them.

" 'He lieth in wait secretly as a lion . . . he lieth in wait to catch the poor'—Psalms, ten. Help! Git this lion off'n me!"

It was Jeremiah Jones, the white-bearded fanatic who preached against horses. Shad controlled his impulse to laugh. He could see the old man was almost scared to death.

"Come here, Tug," he ordered sternly. "Come here and let him up."

The white dog was puzzled but obedient. He took his forepaws off his captive's back and came to stand beside Shad.

The man scrambled to his feet, took one wild-eyed look behind him and started running. His gaunt knees were lifted high and his scarecrow costume flapped behind him as he disappeared in the darkness.

As Shad turned, he saw the single, dusty electric bulb go on in front of the stable. Yance was standing there, peering into the dark.

"Hey!" the gypsy called. "Shad—where are you?"

"Right here," he replied, trying to sound reassuring. "There's nothing wrong, Yance. We had a visitor, but he won't be 'round any more."

As soon as the boy got back to the stable he told his

story. "The poor old coot thought Tug was a lion," he chuckled. "Quoted Scripture to prove it! I never saw anybody worse scared in my life."

But Yance didn't think it was funny.

"You can't tell about crazy people," he said with a frown. "Liable to do anything. What was he doing over here in the dark? Let me have that flashlight an' I'll take a look around."

He beat the grass for two or three minutes before

Shad heard him give a low exclamation.

"What is it?" the boy asked. "Did you find some-thing?"

"Darn right, I did. Look at this!"

He came back to the stable and Shad saw that he was carrying a small, battered kerosene can and half a dozen slips of paper. There was a sloshing noise from the can. It had oil in it.

By the dim glow of the electric bulb they examined the papers. They were tracts—the same kind of printed matter that Jones had been handing out at the grand-stand entrance.

"He must have dropped everything when he heard the dog growl," said Yance. "Don't tell me the guy's harmless. There's only one thing I know of that he'd need oil for, and that's to start a fire!"

It was hard for Shad to believe, but he could think of no other valid reason. "Anyhow," he said, "I'm pretty sure he's through for tonight."

"You go on to bed," the gypsy told him. "I couldn't sleep now if I tried. Soon as I can get hold of Rooney in the morning, I'm going to have Mr. Jones locked up."

.   .   .

Although he had slept little, Yance gave Cedar's Boy his early workout as usual next morning. Shad exer-cised Redwood. He gave him an easy six laps with a half-mile brush at the end. Even with his racing over

for the season he needed to have his training tapered
off gradually.

When the gypsy came back from breakfast he told
Shad he had called the police chief on the phone.
"He'll be over here soon as he picks up our firebug,"
Yance added. "Wants to take a look at the oil can an'
the tracts."

It was nearly nine when the chief's red car came
jouncing in over the turf. He was a beefy, florid-faced
Irishman with an easy-going laugh.

"We got the old codger in for questioning," he told
Yance. "Blamedest story y' ever heard. Says he never
sleeps good in hot weather so he takes walks. He quoted
the Bible at us an' told us how sinful horses was. An'
when we sprung the question about the kerosene on
him he never batted an eye. Guess what he had it for."

Rooney paused, his eyes twinkling. "Seems he can't
stand to have mosquitoes bite him, so he rubs oil on
his face an' hands! I reckon he really does, too, the
way he smelled o' the stuff."

The trainer shook his head, unconvinced. "Maybe
he smells," said he, "but what does that prove? His
story doesn't add up, Chief. There hasn't been a
mosquito 'round here since July!"

The big policeman nodded. "That's right," he said.
"But maybe the old guy don't know it. His head's so
full of his 'work,' as he calls it, I doubt if he notices the
passage o' time. I honestly don't see any grounds for

keepin' him in jail, Yance. But you don't need to worry. We'll watch him close. If he ever acts dangerous we'll get him committed to an asylum. An' just in case I need any evidence, I'll take that oil can along."

Yance was grumpy after the chief had left. "Don't know why cops are so softhearted," he said. "They hate to clutter up their jails, so they're ready to swallow any cock-an'-bull story they hear. I guess we'll just have to stand reg'lar watches an' trust Old Tug to keep the crackpots scared off."

With the trainer in this mood, Shad was somewhat hesitant about asking for time off. However, when he mentioned the pulling match, Yance offered no objections.

"Mr. Martin'll be in pretty soon," he said, "so I've got to stay here any way. You go ahead. Be back at noon."

A good-sized crowd had already gathered around the cleared space back of the Livestock Building when Shad arrived. Most of them were farmers, still interested in good work horses, even though many now owned tractors.

Half a dozen teams were waiting in harness, but he saw no sign of the big drafter from Squantic. He was sizing up the contestants when Bud Martin hailed him.

"See that pair o' grays?" asked the farm boy. "Wait till you get a look at 'em in action! They belong to Cal Hunter, up our way. They're five-year-olds—

Percherons—bred in Iowa. Nineteen hundred pounds apiece!"

"They're a handsome team, all right," Shad agreed. "But there's some other good ones. Look at those bays. Clydes or Shires, I reckon, with all the feathers around their ankles."

"Where's your Squantic mare?" asked Bud, mischievously. "They're about ready to start an' I don't see her. Must have got cold feet at the last minute."

"Search me," said Shad. "Maybe the Mill figured they couldn't spare her on a work day."

There were two men wearing red badges marked *Judge,* talking to the drivers of the teams. One of them walked forward now and addressed the crowd.

"All right, folks," he shouted. "Just step back a little an' make room. We're ready to get this match started. There's five thousand pounds on the stoneboat for the first round. Hitch up that Number One team an' let's go."

The stoneboat was a big wooden drag of smooth, three-inch planks, resting on the ground. The weight consisted of hundred-pound bars of pig iron, piled in rows along its surface. A hook and a heavy chain were attached to the front of the drag.

The first team to try was a pair of big, slow-footed farm-horses, gaunt from the summer's work. One of them, Shad saw, had a swollen hock. Their driver, a lanky, sour-faced fellow from the lower end of the county, made the hook fast to the evener and shook out his whip.

"You've got fifteen seconds to start the load," said the judge. "Have to pull it ten feet. I'll give you the word. You all set? All right—go!"

"Giddap, you!" roared the driver and cracked his whip over the backs of the team. The horses leaned into their collars willingly enough but came up short. The drag failed to move. With an oath the driver hauled back his whip and cut at them viciously, lashing first one, then the other. The result was just what Shad expected. Instead of pulling together the poor beasts made separate forward lunges, jerking the evener back and forth. Finally the off horse—the one with the bad hock—stumbled and fell on his knees.

"Take 'em out!" yelled some of the spectators. "Get a driver that knows his business."

"Time's up," called the judge. And, after a moment's argument, the driver grudgingly unhitched his team.

The hairy-fetlocked Clydesdales were next up. They were handled by a man who understood what he was doing, and the steady power of their pull not only started the drag but moved it the required distance in a few seconds.

Hunter's Percherons performed equally well and one other team managed to qualify within the time limit. These were a pair of tough, wiry lumber-camp horses, driven by a red-headed Irishman. They looked smaller than most of the drafters in the contest but they had plenty of fire and spirit. When they sprang into action the dead weight of the drag went with them.

The judges put down the names of the qualifiers and prepared for the second round. Twenty more bars were added to the load.

"Whew!" said Bud. "Seven thousand pounds! This ought to prove which teams can really pull."

At that moment there was a disturbance beyond the tightly packed ring of spectators.

"Out'my way, dere!" cried a mellow French-Canadian voice. "Geev de Babe a chance!"

Above the heads of the crowd an ominous shape was looming—something that looked as big as a locomotive.

"My gosh!" Bud gasped. "It's a horse!"

"It's Babe!" yelled Shad exuberantly. "Johnny got her here after all!"

The onlookers scrambled out of the way and through the opening they made came the great roan mare, her feet—big over as washbasins—treading slowly and ponderously.

"Hold on, there," called one of the judges. "You're late. The qualifying round's finished an' we've put the weight up a ton. Can't start all over now."

"Hokay," Johnny Couture replied. "Don' tak' no weight off. De Babe, she'll pull her."

The judges held a hasty consultation. They finally

agreed to let the mare pull but said she would have to wait for the last turn.

It was harder work this time. The sturdy Clydes and Hunter's big Percherons made the second pull success-fully, but only after some grunting and straining. The Irish teamster brought his woods nags out and hooked them up.

Their first sharp plunge failed to start the load. He backed them, steadied them for a moment and swung them a little to the left. On that try the stoneboat re-volved a few inches. He pulled the horses to the right and cleverly seesawed the drag until it started, a bare second under the time allowed. Then, with a furious rush, they jerked it onward the required ten feet.

There were some jesting remarks from the crowd as Babe moved into position. "Where'd you get that she-elephant, Frenchie?" one man asked. "She belongs over on the Midway in a side show!"

Johnny grinned and lengthened the draw-chain be-fore hooking it to the mare's massive singletree. At the word he let her lean into the collar to get the feel of the load behind her. Then he began to sing a gay little French tune—*Allouette, gentil allouette*—and slapped the reins on her broad rump.

Babe's hind legs bent a little, then straightened as they took up the strain, and the muscles stood out like cables on her monstrous thighs. Smoothly, almost easily, the drag began to slide ahead. There was no

jerking or plunging. She took a step forward, another
and another, and the job was done.

Johnny was still humming his little tune as he unhitched her, but his voice was lost in a wave of cheers.
The people who crowded around him were popeyed
with excitement. They had seen a marvel—something
they would talk about for weeks to come—a single
horse that could pull as much as a good team!

Cal Hunter, the stocky farmer from up Blue Job
way, looked grim as he watched more iron weights
piled on the stoneboat.

"Seven—eight—nine—ten," Shad counted. "Gosh,
Bud, there's four tons on there now!"

The chunky bays wheeled into position and their
driver faced the judges with a nervous grin. He had a
borrowed whip in his hand.

"Ready?" came the call. "Start pulling!"

The Clydesdales made a gallant try, but the drag
stood still.

"Hi-ya!" yelled the driver and gave them a cut with
the whip. Shad winced at the blow. He knew that was
the wrong way to handle a willing team. They
plunged, lost their footing, jerked unevenly at the
whiffletrees. The seconds ticked by and they were out
of the competition.

Hunter came forward and studied the ground before
he hitched up his Percherons, for the bay pair had
pawed up a lot of turf. When the chain was taut he

talked to the big grays in a low voice, getting them
ready. At last he looked at the timekeeper, got his
nod and shook out the reins.

The horses bowed mightily into their collars. The
traces groaned and creaked. A pebble grated under the
drag and sluggishly the load began to move.

"Now you got it, Prince!" Hunter cried. "Keep her
going, Duke! Hup! Hup!"

It was a magnificent exhibition of power, and the
crowd yelled its appreciation as the big gray team
stood with sides heaving.

The stoneboat had now been pulled so far that only
a dozen yards remained between its square nose and
the wall of the Poultry Building.

"Hold everything," a judge called. "We've got to
unload an' turn around. Give us a hand with that pig
iron, boys."

But Johnny Couture interposed. "Nev' min' dat,"
he told them blandly. "Leave de load on. Babe'll turn
her roun' for you."

The mammoth roan gave a knowing look at the
drag as she was led past. She seemed to be sizing up
the job. Johnny pulled the chain out to one side, at
right angles to the stoneboat, and made fast. He was
crooning again as he gathered the reins. This time the
tune was *Frère Jacques*.

The mare picked up her monstrous hoofs and set
them down, feeling for solid footing. Then she put out

her strength in a real pull. The drag rotated slowly but steadily till it was facing in the opposite direction.

"Hokay?" asked the little Frenchman. "Now we pull?"

The timekeeper, open-mouthed with astonishment, managed to shake his head.

"Not yet," he gasped. "One more team to try first."

Johnny Couture knelt to unhook the chain, but the driver of the lumber-camp team stepped forward and stopped him.

"I'm licked," he said sheepishly. "Hosses just about made it last time an' I don't want to strain 'em. Go ahead, Frenchie. The load's all yours."

"You hear dat, Babe?" sang Johnny. "Le's go, den!"

And once more the mare gathered herself, leaned her great shoulders into the pull and took the stone-boat down the line.

"Somebody pinch me," Bud mumbled. "Am I dreaming, or is there really a horse that strong?"

The judges glanced inquiringly at Cal Hunter. "How much more weight you want to try?" one of them asked.

The farmer looked at his lathered grays and back at the stoneboat. "Reckon I won't try any bigger load," he grinned. "If the mare wants to set a record, more power to her! I'm satisfied just to have the stoutest *pair* in the county."

"How about you, Mr. Couture?"

Johnny was smiling from ear to ear. "Put on all you want," he replied with a lordly wave of the hand. "Me—I got de stoutes' mare in de *worl'!*"

Five more hundred-pound pigs were added to the pile on the drag, while the crowd yelled itself hoarse. If Johnny was singing now, no one could hear him. But the mare must have known. She bowed herself forward half way to the ground, and what had gone before was nothing to this. There was one tremendous explosion of power. The drag surged ahead—traveled not ten feet but ten yards before the little Frenchman pulled Babe to a stop.

Two minutes later he was pinning the big blue winner's rosette to the cheek-strap of her bridle.

THIRTEEN

BUD MARTIN accompanied Shad back to the stable.

"What's this about old Jeremiah Jones?" he asked. "I heard a couple of grooms talking about it."

Shad told him the whole story of the incident, including Chief Rooney's call that morning.

"Well," said Bud, "what do you think, yourself? Was the old geezer really trying to burn us out?"

"Darned if I know," Shad replied soberly. "It sure looked like it when Yance found the kerosene can, but Jones is just nutty enough to use the stuff for mosquitoes, like he said. Yance is worried, an' so am I."

"Dad will be, too, I guess," said Bud. "Our barn got afire once when I was a little kid. The cattle ran out all right as soon as they were let loose, but the horses wouldn't budge. I remember seeing Dad put blindfolds on 'em so he could lead 'em out. He saved all but one—an old work horse named Pete."

"Gosh!" Shad groaned. "A fire in a barn must be an awful thing! I hope I'm never around one. I couldn't stand it to see a horse suffer that way."

They found the Martin horse van standing in front of the stable when they got there. The rear doors were open, the ramp was down and Bud's father was standing beside it.

"I've decided to take Redwood back to the farm," he explained to the boys. "After what happened last night I don't like leaving any more horses around here than I can help. Cedar's Boy has to stay through tomorrow and Saturday, of course, but I'll feel easier when they're all up on Red Horse Hill."

Yance led the blanketed colt out of his stall and tried to coax him up the slope of cleated planks. The young pacer didn't like the idea. He tossed his handsome head, snorted, pawed at the turf and hung back. The hired man who had driven the truck down from the farm made the mistake of attempting to push him from behind and barely dodged a well-aimed kick.

On an impulse, Shad stepped forward. "Do you mind if I try to help?" he asked.

He brought Redwood's currycomb and brush from the stall and went close to his side. Folding back the blanket from the colt's neck, he began gently currying the glossy chestnut coat.

"Like it, don't you, boy?" he said. "M-m-m—feels good, doesn't it?"

He let the young horse sniff at the brush, then took a step up the ramp. "Come on," he suggested in a soothing voice. "Come on with me, an' I'll do it some more."

Slowly he backed up the incline, holding out the brush, and Redwood followed like a lamb. When he was inside the van and his halter rope securely tied, Shad kept his promise. He brushed the colt's sleek hide till it shone like a polished boot.

"I told you this youngster had a way with horses," Yance told his employer. "He's got 'em all so they'd jump through hoops for him."

Hartley Martin chuckled. "I can see that," he said. "I reckon we made a pretty good deal when we hired you, Shad."

The boy felt his face growing hot. He was more pleased than he wanted to show.

"Aw, shucks!" he said. "The colt would have done that for anybody he trusted. I just happened to remember how much he liked to be brushed."

The ramp was pulled up, the doors fastened, and Bud and his father got into the cab with the driver.

"We'll be down early tomorrow to watch Cedar's Boy work," Mr. Martin called. "I'll try to get here by six. An' don't leave the horse alone."

Yance nodded and the van drove off.

"Well," the trainer told Shad with a grin, "looks like we've got just one job now. That's to keep a good watch over Cedar's Boy an' bring him up to race-time feeling right."

"How many more times does he get worked before the race?" Shad asked.

"Only once. I'll give him what we call a blowout tomorrow morning when the boss gets here. That'll be maybe two miles jogging and a good stiff mile on the end of it. He ought to rest about thirty hours before he goes to the post."

Yance sent Shad to lunch early, so that the boy would be back at the stable when he went to get his own mid-day meal at twelve-thirty. The day was hot and still, with an oppressive feel in the air. One of the drivers at the boardinghouse table commented on the weather.

"Thunderstorm's coming sure," he said. "I only hope it holds off till night. I've got a five o'clock race."

When Shad came back to relieve the trainer, he looked into Cedar's Boy's stall. The big bay horse stood drowsing, his eyes half closed, but the skin on his withers twitched occasionally and he shifted his weight from one side to the other. There were no flies in the stall. It must be the heavy air that was making him restless.

The boy found himself a spot where the overhang of the roof gave him shade and went to work on the harness. Tug, stretched out beside him, dozed uneasily in the heat. From the trees beyond the fence came the shrill note of a harvest fly, stabbing the noonday stillness.

A little after one the gypsy returned, and with him was Billy Randall. The old horseman pulled out a rumpled bandanna and wiped his face.

"Close," he said. "Awful close, today. Racin' won't be very good, weather like this. Makes the hosses sluggish."

A piece of paper had dropped from his pocket when he removed the handkerchief. Shad picked it up for him. It was covered with pencil-jotted figures.

"You fellers might be interested in this," the old man remarked. "It's this mornin's odds on the Granite State Stakes. A friend o' mine, Joe Evans, runs a book over to the hotel. He's a square-shooter, an' the authorities leave him alone."

"How are the odds on Cedar's Boy?" Yance asked.

"They suit me," grinned Randall. "He's twenty to one. I got a little piece o' change on him at that figger. There's some others that are better known an' more favored."

He referred to the slip of paper. "That black pacer, Jester, is carryin' the bulk o' the money, at three to one. Next is Mischief Direct. Her odds are five to one. Chansonette's right close—rated six to one. An' the gray trotter I told ye about—Dusty Peter—seems to be well thought of. He's nine to one. Odds'll prob'ly change 'fore race-time. Somebody must ha' been peekin' through the fence at Cedar's Boy. I understand there's some money comin' in on him—nobody knows just where from. Bud ain't a bettin man, is he?"

Yance frowned. "No," he said. "Never heard of him placing a bet in his life. It beats me—unless—"

He turned to Shad. "I s'pose it could be that gang at the Mermaid tent," he mused. "The fellow in the green shirt seemed to be pretty interested in our time."

Shad finished the harness and hung it on its hook. When he returned, Yance and the old trainer had sat down, and Randall was filling a corncob pipe.

"Do you plan to watch the races, Yance?" the boy asked.

"Not me," said the gypsy. "It's more comfortable right here. Why—anything you want to do?"

Shad nodded. "I'd like to have a couple of hours off, if it's all right," he replied. "Maybe it won't take that long."

"Go ahead," said Yance. "Just don't get a heat-stroke."

The boy thanked him and went around the end of the stable. He looked in both directions before making for the fence. It was just as well if nobody saw where he was going.

For twenty-four hours there had been a half-formed plan in the back of his mind. The guilty knowledge he thought he had about the side show "Wild Man" would not let him rest until he made sure, one way or the other. What he would do when he found out he had not yet decided.

Quickly he slipped through the opening where the board was loose and started down the steep bank. Below, half hidden by the alders, he could see the flat-bottomed skiff, tied to a tree. Hank and 'Poleon must be somewhere around the Fair Grounds, though he hadn't seen them that day. His heart was beating fast as he climbed into the boat. He wished the other two

boys were with him, and yet he knew it was better if he shared his secret with no one.

The past few days in the water had swelled the bottom boards, and the skiff leaked very little. He took the oars and pulled quietly out from shore, letting the bow swing downstream. A few moments' rowing brought him around a bend and in sight of Joe Banty's landing. A hundred yards from it he went in to the bank and tied the boat, then went on cautiously afoot.

There was no sign of old Joe among the dahlia plants or down by the dock. Shad climbed the bluff, careful to make no noise, and approached the cabin from the rear. The brush was too thick to give him a view of the shack, but after a few steps he smelled smoke. Crouching, he moved nearer until he could peer out from behind a clump of bushes. A small fire was burning in the littered back yard, and beside it stood the fat old man, barefooted and clad only in overalls as usual.

Shad waited a minute or two, making sure there was nobody else about. He didn't want to startle Joe or make him suspicious. Backing off a little way into the brush he began to whistle carelessly, then came walking out into the clearing with his hands in his pockets.

In spite of the heat the old man looked pale and tense as he stared in the direction of the sound. Even when he made out who his visitor was, Shad thought he seemed uneasy.

The boy strolled up to the fire. "Hi, Joe," he said with a grin. "Trying to keep warm?"

Banty gave a quick glance at the fire and poked at something with a stick. Before the flames consumed it, Shad saw a scrap of something that looked like reddish fur, stained with darker brown spots.

He looked away quickly, trying not to show that he had seen.

"How are things with you?" he asked. "Did that deal for the dahlia go through all right?"

Old Joe relaxed and leaned on his stick. "Not yet," he said. "At least, I ain't got the money. But there won't be any hitch. I've heard from 'em an' they've mailed the check."

"Joe," said the boy, "you said you had to have the cash in a hurry. I don't know what's wrong, but if there's anything I can do—"

The old man gulped and shook his head. "You're a good lad," he answered. "But any troubles I've got are my own. Everything ought to be all right, soon's I get that money."

On an impulse Shad started toward the back door of the cabin. "I've never seen your house," he said. "Mind if I look around?"

"I'd ruther you wouldn't," Joe replied hastily. "I ain't had a chance to clean up or wash the dishes. You come 'round some other time, an' I'll be glad to let you in."

"Okay," said the boy. "Some other time."

He was about to leave when the door opened suddenly and he saw a big, hulking figure standing on the threshold. The man was naked to the waist, but his shoulder and the upper part of one arm were heavily bandaged. From under an unruly shock of red hair his small, scowling eyes peered wildly. His jaw hung down, slack and unshaven.

"Whozat, Paw?" he grunted.

The old man hurried toward him. "It's nobody to be afeared of, Sam. Just a young friend o' mine. You get back inside now."

As the door closed on the apparition, Banty turned

to Shad again, a desperate look on his round, per-spiring face.

"Don't you ever mention this to nobody," he breathed. "That's my boy, Sam. He ain't quite right. Got hurt in a fall a while back an' I'm tryin' to cure him up, but it's a job keepin' him in bed, where he belongs."

"I won't say a thing about it," Shad told him. "Well, so long, now. Hope you get that check in the morning."

He tried to control the trembling in his knees as he went back into the brush. The red-haired half-wit's face had been enough to scare anybody. Angry at himself, he wondered why he had promised Joe not to tell. He had blurted the words out before he thought, and now he was honor-bound to keep his mouth shut.

He went stumbling down the bluff, untied the boat and rowed back up the river. As he crawled through the fence he wished fervently that he had had sense enough to stay away from Joe Banty's place.

FOURTEEN

SHAD could hear the deep-throated roar of the grandstand crowd as he moved toward the stable. He had been gone less than an hour and he wanted time to get his thoughts straightened out before he faced Yance again. Making a wide circuit, he reached the track rail over near the lower turn and found a place where he had a view up the straightaway. A heat had just finished. The trotters were going off the track and the spectators along the rail were mopping their foreheads or fanning themselves with their straw hats. Although a haze now obscured the sun, the air felt more oppressive than ever.

"Don't believe I'll come tomorrow," a man at Shad's side remarked. "Not if it's like this, anyhow."

"It won't be," said his neighbor. "This is a weather breeder. Hear that thunder, off to the west? I doubt if we get home without gettin' wet."

"Guess that's right," the first man agreed. "I'd better

go round up my kids an' get started. See you Saturday, Bill?"

"Oh, sure! I wouldn't miss the big stake race. Got my dough on Jester."

The other man laughed as he turned to leave. "Don't say I didn't warn you," he said. "Mischief Direct's got that one right in her pocket."

Shad leaned there on the rail staring at nothing. True, his promise to Joe Banty gave him an excuse for keeping quiet. But deep in his heart his conscience told him it was only an excuse. The glimpse he had caught of Sam's face still frightened him. Suppose that twisted mind and powerful body went on a rampage. Suppose old Joe or somebody else suffered injury. Wouldn't he—Shad—be to blame?

There was a blurred announcement over the loud-speaker, and he turned with some relief to watch the horses come back on the track. It was a slow class and he was unfamiliar with any of the trotters, but at least they helped to take his mind off the problem that bothered him.

The field scored once, then got off in a cloud of dust. As the horses pounded past him into the turn a long, low rumble of thunder came from the west and he glanced in that direction. It was by pure accident that his eye fell on two moving figures over there among the parked cars. He saw a small man running and dodging, and behind him a heavier man in a green sport shirt, who brandished his fist as if in anger.

It all happened far away and very quickly. In two or three seconds both figures disappeared in the tangle of parked cars. No one else seemed to notice, for the crowd along the track was watching the race. But Shad was sure he had recognized the little man with the pale face and the black hair—the horse-thief, Harko Dan!

The boy left the rail and darted after them. He was out of breath when he reached the place where he had last seen the two men but he kept on, squirming between close-ranked fenders, looking both ways each time he came to an open space. It took him four or five minutes to cross the big parking lot and when he got to the farther side he was completely winded. But the men he was looking for were nowhere in sight.

For a moment he stood there panting, wiping his dripping face on the sleeve of his shirt. The temperature must be close to the hundred mark, he thought. There was no use hunting farther now that he had lost the trail, so he turned, plodding back around the parking space and the grandstand.

At the stable Yance and Billy Randall were still swapping yarns in the shade.

"I think I saw Harko Dan," Shad told them. "He an' that clocker in the green shirt. They were quite a ways off, but it looked like they were having a fight. Anyhow the big guy was chasing the little one. I tried to follow 'em an' lost 'em over in the parking lot."

Yance looked thoughtful. "A fight, eh?" he said. "That's funny. I thought they were in cahoots. If it was really Dan you saw, maybe he was trying to pick the other guy's pocket. That'd be like him. You look all tuckered out, Shad. Better sit down an' rest."

The boy flung himself on a pile of straw, glad to sit still. Most of the sky was overcast now, but the distant thunder seemed to come no nearer.

"How soon do you think it's going to rain?" Yance asked the old trainer.

"Not 'fore night," Randall replied. He squinted at the gloomy sky and sniffed the oppressive air. "This one's goin' to be slow gettin' here, but she'll be a sockdolager when she comes. 'Minds me of a race I druv once in Kalamazoo, Michigan. Squall come up just as we got started. Thunder, lightnin', wind an' rain. One hoss shied at a thunderclap an' tore clean through the fence, an' none of us could see where we were goin'. I won the heat but the judges threw it out— made us trot the whole race over next day."

He rambled on, telling story after story, and Shad listened, half awake. The racing ended and the crowds streamed out of the stands, heading for home. At five-thirty Billy Randall straightened his stiff joints, said good night and limped away.

"You'd better go get your supper," the gypsy told Shad. "It looks more like a storm every minute an' I'd

like to get back here myself before it hits."

The boy went over to the boardinghouse, ate his meal and hurried back. By six-thirty Yance, too, had returned. It was nearly dark now. The black sky in the west was constantly illuminated by flashes of heat lightning and the thunder growled without ceasing.

Yance walked restlessly around the little building. He made sure of the fastening on the half-door of the stall, reset the prop that held the window open, straightened the harness hanging in the tack room.

Cedar's Boy had been fed and watered but he showed no sign of wanting to lie down. He stood quietly enough in one corner of the box. Shad could see the glitter of his eyes every time the lightning flashed.

Even Tug was fidgety. He got up every few minutes to tour the premises. Between times he lay flat on his belly, hind legs stretched out and head on paws, panting steadily. When the thunder rumbled his eyes rolled upward seeking assurance from Shad.

The threatening weather had ruined business at the Fair for that evening. Only a few of the Midway attractions were lighted and the usual milling throng had long since gone home. At eight-thirty Yance shook himself and yawned.

"Shad," he said, "there's no reason why you shouldn't turn in. I'll take the first watch an' you can sleep till one o'clock or so. Then I'll call you an' try to catch a few winks myself. Sequoia's stall's clean. If you go to bed in there, you won't get wet when the rain starts."

Shad gathered up an armful of straw and spread it in the end stall. He left the window and the upper half of the door open for air. Before he went to sleep he saw the light go out in front of the stable and knew that Yance would be sitting there in the dark. He could feel no movement in the heavy atmosphere, but since sunset the heat had become more bearable. Tired, the boy rolled on his side and dozed off.

.   .   .

He had no idea how long he had slept when a blinding glare of lightning and a tremendous thunderclap shook him half awake. There was a wind blowing, snuffing around the eaves and stirring the straw of his bed. The storm—he thought drowsily. It must be coming at last, though as yet there was no sound of rain.

Then he smelled the smoke! It swirled around his head, stinging his eyes and making him cough. The idea flashed across his mind that a bolt of lightning must have struck the stable. Dizzily he sprang to his feet, groping for the door.

"Yance!" he cried, but there was no answer. He stumbled outside. Sparks were shooting up over the roof from the rear of the little frame building. He ran around the end of the stable and saw the back wall of the middle stall already ablaze. The wind was fanning the flames and the dry boards burned like tinder.

"Yance!" he yelled again with the hoarseness of terror in his voice. Then he dashed around to the front once more, wrenched open the door of the red horse's stall and fumbled in the dark for the halter rope. He could hear Cedar's Boy snort with fear, and when he touched the pacer's sweating side it quivered under his hand.

"Steady now, boy," he breathed. "Come on—we've got to get out o' here quick!"

He untied the halter and swung the horse's head toward the door. The smoke was getting thicker now. There was an ominous roaring sound, and a weird red light danced on the ground outside. As they reached the opening Cedar's Boy jerked the rope out of his hand and plunged back into the smoky darkness.

Shad remembered then what Bud had told him about a burning barn. He ran to the tack room and fumbled among the gear till he found a blanket hanging on a peg.

Back in his stall the big horse was cowering against the rear wall, breathing hard and shaking like a leaf. Shad spoke as gently as the strangling smoke would let him.

"We'll be all right in a m-minute, boy," he panted. "Just stand still now."

He worked a corner of the blanket up under the horse's throat and pulled it slowly over his eyes. Cedar's Boy snorted and flung up his head, and Shad had to start over again. The flames had burned through the partition. They were snarling and crackling only a yard away.

The boy ducked low to catch a lungful of air and made a final try. He got the blanket over the horse's head once more and this time, when the big pacer plunged, he hung onto the cloth with both hands. Slowly, foot by foot, he coaxed the fear-crazed animal toward the oblong of flickering light that promised safety.

Even when they were outside he kept the blindfold tightly clutched over the pacer's eyes, for he had heard of horses dashing back into burning buildings. He

led him across the open ground to the end of the big stable and tied him securely to a post.

A man rushed past him shouting the dread word "Fire!" And in a moment the place was alive with swipes and stablehands, hurrying this way and that in complete confusion.

Shad ran back to the blazing structure and wheeled

the sulky and the training cart out of the shed. Yance's driving clothes came next. He reached the harness, hanging on the partition, just as flames began to lick at it. The heat scorched his eyebrows and blistered his face, but he saved the harness before the burning wall toppled outward in a cataract of sparks.

The men from the main stables were forming a bucket brigade as he staggered out. But just as the first dripping pail was passed along the line the rain came. There were no preliminaries. It fell suddenly, in sheets, drowning out the blaze and drenching the fire fighters to the skin. In a minute or two Shad found himself standing in black darkness while the men around him fled for cover.

"Hey!" he shouted, grabbing one of them by the arm. "Have you got a flashlight? Ours was burned up. I've got to find Yance!"

"Come on," the groom told him. "I'll dig one up for you, but let's get out o' this rain."

Shad hurried back with the light. As he passed Cedar's Boy he flashed the beam on him and saw that the horse was standing quietly, head down, with torrents of water sluicing off his back. The boy patted him hastily and ran on. A terrible urgency filled him. He had to find out what had happened to Yance and to Tug.

In front of the ruined stable he halted, shivering, and directed the light into the wet, charred embers.

There was nothing in any of the stalls that could possibly be a body. He moved slowly around to the back, where he thought the fire had started, and his foot kicked against some object that rang like metal. It was an empty kerosene can—the same size as the one Jeremiah Jones had carried!

Shad started to pick it up. Then he remembered there might be telltale fingerprints on it. He left it where it lay and started eastward, following the fence. He had gone perhaps twenty steps when he saw something move in the grass ahead of him.

It was a man and he was trying to lift himself on one elbow. The light glistened on a stained, wet shirt and dungarees, then on a dark, curly head. It was Yance!

As Shad ran up, the gypsy groaned and sank down on his face again. The back of his head was bruised and bloody. The boy got his hands under Yance's armpits and lifted him to a sitting position, trying to steady him.

"Gosh, Yance!" he said, shocked. "What on earth happened?"

The lean face, muddy and blood-smeared, contorted in pain.

"It's my wrist," he mumbled thickly. "When he hit me with that bar—must have broken it."

He jerked suddenly in Shad's arms. "The horse!" he cried out. "Cedar's Boy—is he all right?"

"Yes," the boy told him. "He's all right. Can you walk, Yance? Let's get back there."

Fortunately the trainer wasn't a heavy man. Shad managed to hoist him to his feet and steadied him till his dizziness wore off.

"Somebody set fire to the stable," he told Yance. "But I got Cedar's Boy out—an' the bikes an' the harness."

"Who was it?" Yance demanded. "Who set that fire? Did you get a sight of him?"

"No," the boy replied. "But it was probably the same guy that beat you up. Who was that?"

Yance's voice grated like a file. "I only wish I knew. I owe him something. It was right around midnight that I heard a noise—a kind of choking noise. I thought Tug was in trouble. I ran out back an' saw something white by the fence. Maybe it was the dog. I never found out, because just then I got hit on the head an' knocked down. When I tried to get up somebody was swinging an iron bar at me.

"I guess I put my arm up to protect my face. He must have struck two or three times but I lost count. I was out cold."

He felt gingerly of his left forearm and winced. "If this wrist's busted," he said, "it means I can't drive Saturday."

Shad gaped at him in consternation. "Gee, you're right!" he whispered. "What'll we do?"

Yance shook his head. He was staring at the black-ened ruin that had been the stable.

"Where's the horse?" he asked harshly.

Shad led him over to the corner of the main build-ing, where Cedar's Boy still stood patiently in the rain.

"We've got to get him under cover," said Yance. "Mike Dugan's the stable manager. He'll know if there's a spare stall. But first I'll have to do some 'phoning. I've got to break the news to Mr. Martin."

FIFTEEN

SHAD led the injured trainer along the row of stables to the little office occupied by Dugan. There was a light on, for the stable-boss, roused by the fire, was just preparing to get back in bed. He whistled when he saw Yance's bloody face.

"Faith!" he said. "Ye look like a ghost. Here, sit down an' give me the tale."

Between them they told him what had happened.

"A stall ye need," the Irishman nodded. "An' a stall ye shall have. Number twenty-four's empty. Trotter moved out this mornin'. Put the horse in there an' rub him down good, so he'll take no cold."

"Thanks, Mike," said Yance. "Can I use your 'phone? Shad, you'd better look after the horse."

Shad took Cedar's Boy to his new quarters, found a piece of dry sacking and rubbed him till the dampness was out of his coat. When he was sure the horse was comfortable he picked up the borrowed flashlight and went back to the place where he had found Yance. Tired and wet as he was, he couldn't rest till he knew what had happened to Tug.

He worked along the fence for a hundred yards, then came back slowly, beating through the straggly grass. The rain had stopped falling but everything he touched was sodden and dripping. Several times he called and whistled but the bull terrier gave no answer.

At last, a dozen yards east of the fire-gutted stable, he came on something that might be a clue. It was a piece of raw beef half as big as his fist. He picked it up gingerly, wrapped it in his handkerchief and carried it back to the stable. The big red horse was lying down, breathing slowly and evenly. With a sigh of pure weariness Shad pulled some straw in front of the door, curled up there and went to sleep, wet clothes and all.

The sun was up when he awoke. The stall door was open and Hartley Martin was leaning over him, gently shaking his shoulder.

Shad struggled to sit up. "Gosh, Mr. Martin!" he said. "I guess I overslept. It must be late."

The dairyman smiled. "Not very late, Shad. After what you did last night, I reckon you're entitled to a little sleep. I brought the vet over to look at Cedar's Boy, but he seems pretty healthy to me."

The red pacer was standing a few feet away, nuzzling hungrily at a wisp of hay that had been left in the corner of the manger. Doc Royall came bustling in, took the horse's temperature and felt him up and down.

"He's fit to race right now, if you want," he remarked with a grin. "Outside of a couple of singed hairs in his tail, I'd say he hadn't taken a mite of harm."

Mr. Martin looked relieved. "If he's all right, it's thanks to this lad here," he said. "Yance told me a little over the 'phone, but I'd like to hear the whole story. What about it, Shad?"

The boy recounted the night's events as clearly as he could remember them. "I don't know who did it," he concluded, "but there's something I'd like to show you, down there by the stable."

"We'll wait till Chief Rooney comes," said Mr. Martin. "He ought to be here any minute, but I want to see Yance first, over at Dugan's. If he's able to get up, I'll bring him back with me."

He went off in the direction of the stable manager's office and the vet closed his instrument bag, preparing to leave.

"Doc," said Shad, hesitantly, "if you've got a minute, there's something here I wanted to show you."

He held up the piece of raw meat he had found. "I told you about Tug disappearing—Mr. Martin's bull terrier. An' I wondered if this had anything to do with it. We haven't fed him anything but canned dog food all week."

The veterinarian adjusted his spectacles, examined the meat closely and sniffed at it.

"Couldn't have been there long," he commented. "In that heat yesterday it would've spoiled sure. Has a funny smell—like—hm-m—I've got it. Strychnine! That meat's poisoned!"

"Oh—gee!" Shad whispered. "Poor old Tug!"

"Tell you what," said Royall. "I'll take this back an' get it analyzed. Ought to have the report on it by noon. An' if you come across the dog—or his body—give me a call.

Sorrowfully, the boy went back into the stall and began currying Cedar's Boy. He didn't dare feed him yet, because there was a chance Mr. Martin would want to work him.

In a few minutes the dairyman returned, and with him was Yance. The gypsy looked pale and his head and wrist were bandaged, but he smiled when he saw Shad.

"I hear you had to be waked up," he said. "What kind of a fireman are you?"

The boy grinned. "I never had much experience at it before," he said. "You've had the doctor, haven't you, Yance? What about your wrist? Can you drive?"

"Not today, anyhow. Got to have x-rays taken before I know for sure. But the horse'll have to be worked. Let's look at that harness."

The leather was still damp from the rain, but it had been well oiled only the day before, and felt pliable enough.

"I reckon it's all right," was the trainer's verdict. "Roll out the bike, an' hitch him up."

Shad looked at him in surprise. "You mean the racing sulky?" he asked.

"Yep. The boss wants to see a real time trial."

Shad's heart beat faster. Maybe he would handle Cedar's Boy in the workout—unless Mr. Martin decided to take the reins himself. He wheeled out the light racing bike and wiped off the seat and frame, stained by the downpour.

"Never mind that," Yance told him. "Track's going to be muddy anyhow. Get the harness on him."

Three minutes later the big horse was in the shafts and every buckle in place. Shad hooked the checkrein and stood by, waiting for orders.

"All right," said Yance, "you're up. You won't have the watch this time. We'll keep that here. Want to see how good a natural judge o' pace you are. How about those last two laps, Mr. Martin?"

"I'd like about two-twelve," the owner replied, "if he'll do it without pushing. Can't tell yet how much last night took out of him. Take him four laps at a jog an' then bring him down pacing. We'll be at the finish line."

Shad's head was in a whirl as he climbed aboard the sulky. Two-twelve. How was he going to tell.

"Here—you'll need goggles when you get out in that mud," said Yance. "An' carry the whip but don't use it. That's it. Now, by jingo, you look like a driver!"

The sun was bright and the air cool and bracing after the storm. Shad could feel the pacer's eagerness through the reins. Once on the track he had to steady him by voice and hand to keep him at the easy, rocking, warm-up gait.

They were lucky to have the oval to themselves. The

other trainers would probably wait till the surface dried out and the scrapers did their work. Shad kept well to the outside, going the wrong way of the track. The mud was an inch or two deep but it didn't seem to bother Cedar's Boy.

As they came around on the fourth lap, Shad looked toward the rail opposite the judge's stand and caught a nod from Yance. He took the horse up to the head of the stretch, pulled him down to a walk and turned him. The big bay's ears pricked up expectantly. He knew what this meant.

Shad settled himself on the seat, braced his feet and took a firm grip on the hand-loops. He could just about see over the pacer's rump when the horse was walking. Now, as Cedar's Boy began to pace, the long red body lowered and flattened out, so that Shad had a better view of the track. He edged the horse over toward the pole and brought him down—not too fast—to the starting line.

"Go!" shouted Hartley Martin. The boy lifted the reins a little and Cedar's Boy responded with a rush. Twenty yards beyond the line he was going like a breeze. Two-twelve, Shad thought. How fast was that? He wasn't going quite fast enough, he decided, but he'd save the real speed for the second lap.

Clods of mud had begun to fly from the pacer's feet, spattering Shad's chest and face. Once or twice he had to wipe the goggles by bending his head and rubbing them on the shoulder of his shirt.

On the backstretch he stepped up the pace a notch, for he could feel that the big horse had plenty in reserve. They spun around the upper turn and Cedar's Boy was fairly flying as they came down toward the stands.

Shad had a blurred glimpse of the two faces by the rail. The next moment something happened. There was a clink of metal and the easy power went out of the pacer's gait. He half stumbled, recovered himself and tried gallantly to get going again, but Shad could feel him limping. In a panic, the boy steadied him, talked to him, finally eased him down to a jerky walk before they reached the curve.

Shad was almost in tears. Uncertain what to do, he turned the horse and brought him to a stop near the outer rail. Mr. Martin was coming on the run. His face was gray with alarm when he reached them.

"You'd better get down, son," he panted. "What happened? Did he throw a shoe?"

"I don't know," said Shad miserably. "I heard something that sounded like a loose shoe and then he stumbled."

The dairyman unhitched the checkrein and let the pacer's head down. Stooping, he took a gentle grip on the right forefoot and lifted it.

"That's it, all right," he said with obvious relief. "Lost the plate. I think you got him stopped in time and there's no real damage done. Lead him back to the stable, Shad, and I'll go and see the blacksmith."

Shad took the bridle and laid an affectionate hand on the big bay's silky nose. "Don't feel bad, boy," he murmured. "We'll get that foot fixed up an' you'll be going fast as ever."

He led the horse slowly up the track. A few yards from the judges' stand he picked up a light crescent of steel that was half buried in the mud. It was a racing plate.

.   .   .

Big John O'Brien had a reputation as the best shoer of harness horses in New England. His huge truck, with its two forges and a glittering array of racing shoes in all weights and sizes, was a regular feature of the county fair circuit.

It wasn't one of his helpers but Big John himself who came to the stable to look over Cedar's Boy. He felt of the pastern and frog with knowing fingers, and examined the whole hoof critically.

"Good thing it didn't happen in a race," he grunted. "Another lap on this an' he might ha' been out of it for a year. Let's see that old plate, sonny. Hmm, made this one myself. Okay, let him stand in the stall. I'll bring the truck over in an hour or two."

Shad felt better when he had put away a plate of ham and eggs and hot biscuits. He came back from the boardinghouse to find Chief Rooney talking to

Mr. Martin and Yance in front of the stable.

The policeman turned to Shad. "Hi, young feller," he said. "Sounds like quite a night's work you put in. What happened? Lightnin' strike the place?"

"No," the boy answered. "Leastways, I don't think so. I think it was set afire. There's something back there I want you to see."

He led the way down past the spot where the little stable had stood and pointed to the oil can lying in the grass.

"That's right where I found it last night," he said. "Hasn't been touched. I thought maybe you could find fingerprints on it."

The Chief nodded. "We'll check that," he said.

"Looks like that old scamp Jones was mixed up in it, don't it? Reckon I never should ha' let him out when I had him in jail. Did you find anything else?"

"Yes." Shad gulped and looked at Mr. Martin. "I'm afraid old Tug's done for," he said sadly. "I picked up a chunk o' raw meat over near the fence. Doc Royall thinks it's poisoned. He's having it tested."

Chief Rooney scowled. He was a tenderhearted man under his gruff exterior, and he didn't like dog-poisoners.

"More evidence against Jones," he snapped. "Had cause to hate the dog, didn't he?"

"Hold on, Chief," Yance put in. "I don't think it was Jones. The fellow that laid me out was strong, an' mean, an' quick on his feet. I didn't get a real look at him, it's true. But I sure would have noticed that flopping white beard."

The Chief looked thoughtful. "There's one possibility I'd forgot," he mused. "That's the Wild Man. We found out from Maguire who he is. Joe Banty's son, Sam. I'm meetin' the sheriff in half an hour an' we expect to round him up. Joe's shack's only a mile downriver. He could ha' been the one."

"While you're listing the suspects," said Hartley Martin, "I'd like to drop one more name in the pot. Don't forget Harko Dan. He's still loose, and I think he'd take some pretty long risks to get even with Yance and me."

Chief Rooney laughed. "I'll take him into account," he replied. "But I've begun to think that gypsy's just a myth. We ain't got a bit of actual proof he's within a hundred miles o' here."

"It was the dog poison made me think of him," said Mr. Martin. "He's that kind."

The Chief bade them good-by and drove off. A few minutes later they were joined at the stable by Billy Randall. Shad went to get a pail of water for Cedar's Boy. When he came back, the old trainer was apparently answering a question.

"Nope. Not me, Bud," he said. "Ain't been up on a sulky for years, an' the rheumatiz' in my wrists is so bad I couldn't hold a Shetland pony, let alone a real handful o' hoss."

Mr. Martin looked glum. "I don't know where we'll find a driver then," he said.

"Used to be pretty fair at it, yourself," the old man answered with a twinkle in his eye. "But if you don't want to drive, you can find a good 'un without lookin' very far."

"Where?" asked the dairyman quickly.

"Right here," Randall told him, and before the astounded Shad could move, the old trainer clapped a hand on his shoulder.

SIXTEEN

RANDALL beamed at the others. "Who do you reckon knows the hoss better'n anybody else 'cept Yance?" he challenged. "This boy here. Who got him out o' that fire alive an' still sassy? Shad did. I've watched him drive. He's got grit an' hoss-sense. An' he's got hands. Maybe he won't win—but he'll let 'em all know they was in a race. After all, I'm bettin' my own money on Cedar's Boy, an' I'm satisfied to see Shad holdin' the lines."

Yance looked at his employer and nodded. "Billy's right," he said. "The boy could do it. What was the time for that first lap? One-seven-an'-a-half? You said yourself he'd judged the pace better'n if he'd had the stop watch."

"That's true," Mr. Martin agreed. "But there may be some tricky driving in the Free-for-All. It's a big field. I'd rather have a man in there who knows all the dodges. Besides—Shad hasn't a license to drive in a race."

"I'd thought o' that," said the old trainer. "I know the officials pretty well an' I reckon we can get him one. They'll take my word. As far's the tricky drivin' goes, I've got time to learn him a few things about keepin' out o' trouble."

Shad held his breath as he watched Hartley Martin's face. At last the dairyman's brow cleared as he made up his mind.

"All right, Billy," he grinned. "You win. But you've taken on quite a responsibility. It's only about thirty hours to race-time."

Randall straightened his bent back. "I ain't worried," he said. "Come on, Shad. You an' me's got some talkin' to do."

The old fellow led him over to the track and they leaned on the rail, close to the head of the straightaway. The mud was drying out fast and the scrapers were already at work.

"She'll be ready for the afternoon card, all right," said Randall. "We'll watch all the races, an' I can point out things to you then. But the main thing to remember is this: the best driver in the world is the feller that knows all the tricks so good he never has to use 'em."

For more than an hour the old driver talked steadily, drawing on the immense fund of experience he had gained in half a century on the tracks. Shad didn't need a notebook. The idea of driving Cedar's Boy in the Granite State had been frightening at first. Now he was filled with a fierce determination to do the job right. Nothing the old man told him could be lost or forgotten. He stored up every word in his memory, and if there was anything he didn't understand he asked questions until he had the answer.

The tractors moved off the oval and a few horses appeared. One of them was a big black pacer, sleek and shining in the morning sun.

"That's Jester," said Randall. "He's the favorite. Good hoss, too. Placed second in a two-four heat in a pacin' stake out at Delaware, Ohio. Luke Benton's goin' to drive him. I wouldn't say he's the smartest feller I know, but he's done pretty good on the Grand. Look, here comes a couple more. See that nice-goin' brown mare? She's the Maine pacer I was talkin' about— Mischief Direct. Ken Wicks up, an' he's what I'd call a first-class driver.

"The long-legged gray hoss comin' 'round the curve now is Dusty Peter. Don't he look like the pictures o' Greyhound? That's one you got to watch. He may look awkward but with that reach he's got speed."

At eleven o'clock Randall took his pupil over to the office of the U. S. Trotting Association. Hartley Martin was there, and Yance. The man at the desk eyed Shad keenly as he shook his hand.

"Think you've got muscle enough to hold a big

horse on a break?" he asked.

Shad met his searching glance steadily. "Cedar's Boy won't break," he answered. "But if he should I can hold him."

The official turned to Martin with a nod. "It's a bit irregular," he said, "but under the circumstances, I think we can give him a license. Billy Randall's a pretty fair judge of drivers."

When they left, Shad had the precious bit of paper in his pocket.

He went to lunch with the old trainer at the horsemen's boardinghouse, but he was too excited to have much appetite. As they came out and started in the direction of the stables, Shad caught a glimpse of the man in the green shirt. He was a hundred yards away and walking fast, as if in a hurry to get somewhere.

"Mr. Randall," said the boy hastily, "I've got an errand to do. It won't take long. I'll be back in ten or fifteen minutes. Do you mind?"

He darted off toward the grandstand, where the clocker had disappeared around the corner. A moment later he had him in view again. The man was moving rapidly past the end of the track, heading for the Midway. This time he didn't go to the Mermaid tent. As he passed the tattered cloth sign that advertised Ki-Ko, the Wild Man, he looked around furtively and ducked under the canvas at the side.

Since Sam Banty's escape the show hadn't been open.

Shad was certain now that the bookies had moved their base of operations. He sauntered slowly past, circled another concession and came back toward the rear of the Ki-Ko tent, moving as silently as he could. There was nobody in sight when he flattened himself on his stomach, a foot from the canvas.

Inside he could hear a mumble of voices. He recognized the gruff tones of the husky fellow in the green shirt, and strained his ears to catch the words.

"Yeah," the man was saying. "He was tryin' to double-cross us all right—the dirty little weasel. Only it didn't work. They saved the hoss. I seen him workin' out this mornin'. Lost a shoe, but he'll be fit to race. Dunno what they'll do for a driver, though, with the gypsy hurt. Maybe we'd better hedge that bet."

"What with?" the other voice snarled. "I ain't got any more dough, an' neither have you. Wait till I catch that sneakin' jailbird!"

Shad had heard enough. He crawled away, got to his feet and ran up the Midway. There were half a dozen telephone booths in a building near the entrance, and he found one of them empty. The police

number was on the back of the directory. He dropped
in his nickel and dialed it with shaking fingers, and in
a moment he was asking for Chief Rooney.

"Rooney, Chief o' Police, Riverdale," came the answer.

"Chief," the boy panted, "this is Shad Davis—you
know—stableboy for Mr. Martin."

"Yep. I remember. What's botherin' you, Shad?"

"I located that bookie joint. It's in the back o' the
Ki-Ko tent, where the Wild Man show was. I listened
an' heard 'em talking. If you want Harko Dan, I think
maybe they know where to find him."

He gave the policeman the conversation, word for
word as nearly as he remembered it.

"Sounds like a real lead," Rooney commented. "I'll
have some men there right away. If we pick 'em up I
reckon they'll talk, an' that sort o' settles the question
about who set the fire. Thanks, sonny. See you later."

Much as he wanted to wait for the arrival of the
police, Shad was a boy of his word. He had told Randall
he'd be back in fifteen minutes and he would have to
hustle to make it.

When he reached the stable he was glad he had run. The old trainer pulled a big silver watch out of his pocket and checked the time. "Quarter of an hour on the nose," he commented. "Yance says you're a good judge o' pace an' I guess he's right. Let's go over to the paddock an' watch 'em hitch up for the first race."

Randall didn't introduce Shad to the other drivers. There was time enough for them to find out for themselves that he was going to handle Cedar's Boy. And since they paid little attention to the tall, thin youngster, he was able to watch them and listen to their talk almost as if he had worn a cloak of invisibility.

There was one man in the group whom he disliked from the start. That was Jake Jarvis, the driver who had nearly caused a spill on opening day. He was cocky and loudmouthed and he constantly needled the other reinsmen.

Randall was chewing a straw as he sauntered toward Jarvis' sulky. "Hear you're up behind the Felton mare tomorrer, Jake," he remarked. "How's she go?"

"Oh, so-so," said Jarvis. "Nothin' to get excited about. Just a fair turn o' speed."

His eyes had narrowed a little at the question, and Shad thought he had seemed almost too indifferent in his reply. The old trainer made no comment until they were out of earshot. Then he winked at the boy.

"I thought so," he said. "Jarvis has got a fast trotter an' he knows it. Never heard him miss a chance to brag before. They're tryin' to keep her dark, but I'd watch out for that Chansonette if I was you."

They stood by the track rail all that afternoon. There were five races on the card, and as he listened to Billy Randall's pithy comments, Shad learned something from every one.

He learned that smart horsemen didn't always try to steal the pole on the start; that you could save your horse by getting in behind the pole sulky and letting the leader cut down wind resistance; that the best time to make your move was coming off the curve into the backstretch, but it might be at a dozen other points depending on circumstances.

"Matter o' fact," the old driver told him, "no two heats was ever just alike. You got to have an instinct inside you that tells you what to do an' when to do it. Partly, it's the way the hoss feels about it. Cedar's Boy's got sense, like his grandpaw. He'll let you know. An' if I didn't think you had the gift to understand him, I wouldn't be wastin' time on you. My leg an' back are mighty stiff from standin' here now."

In spite of his discomfort, the old man stuck it out till the last race was finished and the winner posted. Then he hobbled back to the stable with Shad at his side.

Yance was sitting there with the harness across his knee, trying to clean it with one hand. Shad hurried to take it from him, full of remorse.

"I'm awful sorry, Yance," he said. "I was so busy trying to remember everything I heard that I forgot all about the stable work."

The gypsy laughed. "Well," he replied, "you're goin' to be the driver, so I guess that makes me the swipe. You able to teach him anything, Billy?"

"Hard to say." The old trainer winked at Shad. "What I give him today a man gen'ally has to learn in twenty years o' steady drivin'. I reckon no youngster ever growed up any faster'n Shad did this afternoon."

The boy finished washing and oiling the harness, then wiped down the sulky and polished the steel wire spokes. He was putting away the rags and bottles when he heard Hank Wetherbee's voice outside.

"Where'll I find the Martin stable?" he was asking.

"Martin?" came the reply. "Oh—they're the folks that got burned out. You'll find 'em in number twenty-four. You're just about back of it now."

As he stepped outside, Shad saw Hank and 'Poleon coming around the corner. The French boy was carrying something in his arms—something heavy and white.

"Here, Shad," said he, sober-faced. "We've got your dog."

Yance got up quickly. Together they stared at the inert white shape as 'Poleon laid it on the ground.

"Gosh! Is he—" Shad hesitated, hating to say the word. But Tug answered his question for him. Slowly the dog lifted his head, then rolled over and, with a struggle, got his forelegs under him. Stretching out his muzzle he gave the boy's hand a feeble lick.

"We found him down in the woods, below the fence," Hank explained. "We were on our way to get the boat an' start home. He was headed down hill an' his tongue was out—looked like he was tryin' to crawl to the water. He can't move his hind legs at all. What happened? Somebody run over him?"

"No," said Shad with a choke in his voice. "He was poisoned, I think. Poor old Tug! Are you thirsty?"

"We gave him some water," said 'Poleon. "Took him right down to the river. Boy—he sure wanted it!"

"Thanks, boys," said Yance. "Mr. Martin's goin' to be mighty grateful to you. Shad, you'd better get over to Dugan's office an' put in a call for Doc Royall."

The boy set off at a run. He found the vet was out but he left word that Tug had been found and was still alive. He knew Royall would come as soon as he got the message.

Hank and 'Poleon had stayed to learn more about the fire, and Shad found he was a hero when he returned. The boys stared at him admiringly and plied him with questions, much to his embarrassment. Finally he convinced them they would be late for supper if they didn't start home, and accompanied them as far as the fence.

"I found out yesterday," he told them, "who the Wild Man is. It's Joe Banty's half-wit son. I went down there and Joe was trying to hide him. He probably thinks I told the police, but I didn't. They got it from the guy that runs the Ki-Ko show. I'd hate to have the old man hold it against me, so if the cops or the sheriff have been there after him, tell Joe how it was, will you?"

They were halfway down the bluff when he ran back and called to them through the fence.

"One thing more," he said. "Stop by my house an' ask Dad an' Mother to be sure to come to the races tomorrow. Tell 'em I'm going to be awful disappointed if they aren't here."

"Why?" asked Hank.

"Never mind why. Just give 'em that message an' make it as strong as you can."

Hank laughed. "Okay," he answered. "We'll tell 'em. Sounds kind o' mysterious, though. Maybe we'd better be up in the stands, too."

"Sure," said Shad. "The more the merrier." And he strutted back to the stable feeling seven feet tall.

SEVENTEEN

THE sight of Yance, bending over the helpless bull terrier, brought Shad back to earth in a hurry. Tug was thin, and his white coat, usually so immaculate, was muddy and unkempt.

While they waited for the veterinarian, the boy got a sponge and a bucket of water and cleaned him off as gently as he could. Tug was still thirsty. Shad placed a shallow pan of water within reach and he lapped at it every few minutes.

At six o'clock Yance went to supper. Billy Randall had left earlier, with a promise to be back. Shad gave the horse his evening feed and sat down with the dog. After a few minutes he heard the chug and rattle of an ancient car. Doc Royall's little coupé wheezed to a stop and he got out.

"Still alive, eh?" he asked briskly. "That's good news. Maybe we can pull him through. Here, old fellow, let's have a look at you."

When he finished his examination he got some capsules out of his bag and persuaded the dog to swallow one.

"I was over at Collins' drugstore when you called up," he told Shad. "They'd just finished the analysis on that meat. It was strychnine, sure enough. I'd have known it from the dog's symptoms. Paralysis of the hind legs—that's normal in strychnine cases. What I hope is that he didn't eat too much of it. You'll want to keep him warm tonight. Better wrap him in a horse blanket an' lay him inside—maybe over in the corner of the horse's stall. That's about all we can do for him except wait. I'll come 'round again in the morning."

Yance came back soon after Doc Royall had left, and he, too, was cheered by the news that Tug had a chance for recovery. Together they made the bull terrier as comfortable as they could, then came out to sit in front of the stall. Shad had forgotten all about supper, and had to be urged to go before the boardinghouse closed.

"I know how you feel," Yance told him. "I was the same way before my first race. But you're goin' to need all your strength tomorrow. Get over there right now an' eat hearty."

There was quite a group around the stable when he returned at dusk. He saw Hartley Martin's car, and Chief Rooney's. Bud Martin was there, as well as Billy Randall, and there was still another man—a big young fellow with close-cropped blond hair.

"Shad," said the Chief, "I want you to meet Tom Burke—'Tiger' Burke, they used to call him when he played tackle for State. Tiger, this is Shad Davis."

"Hi, Shad," the ex-football player grinned, and thrust out a powerful hand.

"Tiger's a cop now, an' a good one," Rooney explained. "I've assigned him to stay here with you tonight, in case there's any more trouble."

"Trouble?" asked the boy.

"Oh, it ain't likely anything'll happen," said the Chief. "Only we're pretty sure now the fire last night was a grudge job. We got those two small-time gamblers you tipped us off to. They talked, all right. Told us Harko Dan was in their gang but they had a bust-up when he found they'd put some money on Cedar's Boy. Last they saw of him, he told 'em the hoss'd never start the race.

"They gave us an address where we could find him," he added. "Hoped to collect the reward, I guess, but he'd skipped out 'fore we got there. Harko Dan's our man. We'd already eliminated the other suspects. Ol' Jerry Jones was in bed at his roomin' house all night—snorin' so loud nobody else could sleep."

"What about Sam Banty?" Shad asked.

Rooney shook his head. "I never did think he was mixed up in it," he said. "Pore harmless critter! When the sheriff an' I got to Joe's place, he was there all right. Joe'd got some money from sellin' a dahlia plant, an' he had Sam dressed up in a new store suit, ready to take him off to a private institution.

"I sort o' persuaded the sheriff that he didn't have any charge against the feller, except maybe vagrancy, an' the county'd have to pay for his keep if he locked him up. He agreed that farmer had been a mite hasty with his gun, an' the best way was to let the whole thing drop."

The Chief chuckled. "Matter o' fact," he said, "the sheriff loaned Joe a car an' a driver to take Sam to the sanitarium!"

"You don't think he was really dangerous, then?" asked Hartley Martin.

"Shucks, no! I've known him since he was a kid. He never was crazy—just weak in the head. Way I figger, what little brains he had got sort of addled, bein' cooped up in that durn cage, wearin' a mangy fur suit an' havin' raw meat shoved at him with a pitchfork. 'Nough to make anybody desperate after a while. So Sam just pulled the bars apart an' headed for home."

Bud Martin had been waiting to get Shad off by himself. Now he took his arm and pulled him to one side.

"I've been about busting to talk to you ever since Dad told me," he grinned. "Boy—what a thrill! How do you feel—nervous?"

"Yes, kind of," said Shad. "It's like getting up to recite poetry in front o' the class, only ten times worse.

Billy Randall's been coaching me, though. If I can remember all he's told me, maybe I'll make out."

"Sure you will! Uncle John Mason says he knew you were a natural-born driver the first time he set eyes on you. He wants to come down tomorrow, an' Aunt Sarah, too. O' course Dad an' Mother'll be here. Do your folks know?"

Shad shook his head. "Not yet. I'm scared they wouldn't let me drive. But I sent word there was a special reason why they ought to come."

Chief Rooney had already left, and now Mr. Martin called his son.

"Come on, Bud," he said. "Time we were getting home. Get some sleep, boys, but take good care o' the horse. We'll see you in the morning."

When they had driven away, Billy Randall lighted one of his stogies and puffed thoughtfully for a while.

"One thing we got to do," he said, "is figger what Shad's goin' to wear tomorrer. Think your clothes'll fit him, Yance?"

"I thought o' that," the trainer replied. "They were pretty well mussed up with the smoke an' the rain so I had 'em cleaned an' pressed today. Let's try 'em on, Shad."

The boy was a little taller than Yance, and somewhat slimmer in the waist. He worked his legs into the sand-colored moleskins and found they were only an inch or two short at the ankles.

"That won't hurt," said Randall. "Pull the belt tight an' let 'em hang low on your hips. Now, what about the jacket?"

Shad had enough breadth of shoulder to fill the blue sateen blouse snugly. "Gee," he said, "it's perfect! An' I know the cap'll fit, because I tried it on once—just to see how it'd feel to be a driver."

Billy Randall laughed. "You must ha' had second sight," he commented, "lookin' ahead to this. Well, you're all set now. A little polish on your boots an' you'll be as smart as any of 'em—in looks, that is."

The boy removed his finery and they sat talking for another hour. Young Burke was modest about his football exploits. Instead of discussing them, he listened in delight while Billy Randall drew on his inexhaustible fund of harness horse stories.

Shad's eyelids began to droop and he caught himself yawning once or twice. Yance, too, was tired.

"Here," the gypsy said at length, "we don't want Shad fallin' asleep in the sulky tomorrow. Time to turn in. They've got a cot for me at Dugan's, so I'll say good night."

"All right," chuckled Randall. "I can take a hint. I know when my company ain't wanted. So long, folks." And he went limping off into the dark.

Their present stable quarters included the box stall and a combined tack room and sulky shed. The young policeman placed a box just inside the shed and sat down on it.

"I'll be able to keep awake," he told Shad. "Had plenty of experience at it, doing guard duty in the Army. If anybody comes around, I'll be back in here where they won't see me. Sort of hope they do come. I'd like to catch this Harko Dan character."

Shad took a look at Tug and tucked the blanket around him tightly. The dog's breathing was steady and his nose was no longer hot and feverish. The boy refilled his water pan, then made himself a bed of straw and lay down lengthwise across the stall door.

Cedar's Boy was asleep and dreaming. Occasionally Shad heard him sigh and his legs twitched a little, rustling the straw. The boy's own dreams were of racing, too. He could feel the pull of the reins and hear the thunder of shadowy hoofs. Villainous-faced drivers tried to box him or crowd him. Disaster was always close. But by miracles of coolness and daring he warded off one threat after another.

·   ·   ·

It wasn't a sound that woke him but a hardly perceptible draft of cool air. The door was opening silently above him, and against the night sky a dark figure loomed. A man was coming into the stall!

Before Shad could move or cry out, the intruder tripped over him and sprawled forward. He was on his feet again like a cat—up and moving while the boy was still scrambling to his knees.

"Tiger!" yelled Shad, and dove blindly for the man's legs. It was a lucky tackle. He brought his opponent down with a crash, and for breathless seconds they struggled on the straw-covered floor. Then a light went on. Someone jumped across Shad's body and there was a hollow thumping sound. The man's legs stopped squirming and the fight was over.

Shad looked up to see Tom Burke towering over him, a blackjack in his hand.

"Well, I'll be!" grunted the policeman. "Look at that, will you?"

The boy staggered to his feet. On the floor lay the pale-faced, black-haired man he had expected to see. But the man's right hand, gripping a long, shiny knife, was firmly pinned down by a pair of powerful jaws. Tug, eyes half closed and a kind of grim smile on his face, had kept that lethal blade out of action!

Somehow, in Shad's moment of need, the dog had twisted his body around and locked his teeth on the intruder's wrist.

The man was unconscious from Burke's blow on the head. The policeman took the knife from his inert fingers and turned to Shad.

"Who is this guy?" he asked.

"I think he's Harko Dan," said the boy, and shivered. He was beginning to realize how close he had come to being stabbed. "You keep him here," he added, "an' I'll go get Yance. He'll know."

The trainer growled when Shad tried to wake him, but as soon as his mind grasped the boy's excited words he was out of his cot with a bound.

"A knife, eh?" he said as he pulled on his trousers. "That's like the dirty rat. He'd have slit the horse's throat if he hadn't fallen over you first."

Once they reached the stable it took Yance only a moment to identify his old enemy. He ran his fingers inside the man's shirt and fished out a strange-looking yellow coin on a string.

"It's Harko Dan," he said flatly. "That's the gypsy charm he used to wear. Look at his ears, too. Pierced for earrings. You can make it positive when you check his fingerprints."

Gently they loosened Tug's jaws, and the dog rolled over and went to sleep again. Burke put handcuffs on the prisoner, then doused him with cold water to bring him to.

The man's eyes opened. He glared at them sullenly but said nothing.

"What's your name?" snapped Burke.

There was no answer.

"Okay," said the policeman, and jerked him to his feet. "Mind putting through a call to the station, Shad? Tell 'em to send a car."

The boy ran back to Dugan's office and dialed the police number. The desk sergeant answered sleepily but sounded wide enough awake when Shad told him the news.

Even before he returned to the stable he heard the far-off wail of a siren, and a few minutes later a police car came rocketing through the Fair Grounds, its headlights glaring on the walls of tents and buildings.

Burke dragged his prisoner out and bundled him into the rear seat. As the car started up he waved to Yance and Shad.

"Guess you won't need me any more tonight," he called. "You'll be hearing from the Chief in the morning."

The trainer yawned. "Well," he said, "that's that. I reckon you can really sleep now, Shad. You've earned it. An' don't bother about gettin' up early. You can lie as late as you like."

The boy turned off the light and lay down again. For some reason his nerves were no longer taut and jumpy. The struggle with Harko Dan had released some of his energy. He stretched luxuriously in the straw and slept, this time with no dreams to bother him.

He woke up when Cedar's Boy whinnied. The horse was pawing the floor and acting hungry, and the sun was well up in the sky.

Shad brushed the straws out of his hair and washed himself at the spigot. He brought a pail of water for Cedar's Boy, gave him his usual feed and curried his rumpled flanks while the horse munched his oats and bran.

Over in his corner, Tug woke and yawned. When Shad looked toward him he was amazed to see him standing on all four feet. The dog gave a little whimper and advanced several wobbly steps before his hind legs caved under him.

"Good boy!" cried Shad, hurrying to his side. "I believe you're really getting better. An' gosh—am I thankful you were here last night!"

He was sitting with Tug's head in his lap when Yance appeared in the doorway. The gypsy's hawklike face softened.

"How is he?" he asked huskily.

"Better," said Shad. "He was up an' walked a little, just now."

Yance grinned. "Good enough," he said. "But it's

near eight o'clock an' you won't get any breakfast if you don't hustle over there. I'll look out for Tug. Doggone it, boy, do you know what day this is? It's Big Saturday! It's race day!"

EIGHTEEN

AFTERWARD, when Shad tried to recall all that happened that morning, his memory was blurred. He knew he ate a good breakfast. But when he got back to the stable it seemed as if everybody wanted to talk to him at once. Chief Rooney, jubilant over the capture of Harko Dan, clapped him on the back and praised him over and over again. Hartley Martin was equally pleased but didn't talk as much. The veterinarian came to see Tug, promising a quick recovery. And Big John O'Brien made a final check on all four of the pacer's shoes, including the new front plate. Both of them stayed to gossip and make admiring comments on Shad's adventure.

Yance and Billy Randall had a good many bits of last-minute advice to give the boy, and his head whirled as he tried to store all of it away.

Finally he escaped into the big bay's stall. There, with no voices ringing in his ears, he spent a long time currying and brushing the horse. It was a relief to tell him all about the race—how he felt about it—how much he was depending on Cedar's Boy's courage and speed to pull them through. He didn't need to put all this in words. His thoughts passed through his fingers and he was sure the pacer understood.

Noon came and he found himself at a table, with Billy Randall trying to coax him to eat. He did manage to swallow about half a bowl of soup, but that was all.

"I've got a funny feeling in my stomach," he told the old trainer unhappily. "Something like butterflies."

"Yeah," said Randall. "I know. Used to have 'em myself. Good thing before a race. But you'll get over it, soon as you cross the startin' line."

They came out into the midday sunshine and the noise and confusion of Big Saturday. Fifty thousand people jammed the Fair Grounds that day—three or four times the normal population of Riverdale. They had poured in from many miles around, in new cars, old cars, trucks and farm wagons. The clamor of their voices, the shouts of the barkers and the music of calliopes blended into a wave of sound that was unlike any other on earth.

Already there was a scattering of people in the grandstand. Some had eaten their lunches. Others carried food with them in shoe boxes and paper bags. Now, above the din, there was a rising throb of drums,

and the Riverdale Band came marching across the infield, looking hot and uncomfortable in heavy blue
uniforms.

The boy and the old man came in sight of the stable.
"Oh, gosh!" Shad breathed. "There are my folks! I

was hoping they wouldn't see me till I was out on the
track."

"You keep a stiff upper lip," Randall whispered. "If
I was your dad I'd be prouder'n a banty rooster."

Shad's mother must have heard the news. She looked
pale, and her lips were tightly set. But when she saw
him she smiled a little.

"Gee, Ma," he blurted, "you sure are a knockout in
that new dress. How's everything at home?"

"Melvin," she replied, "don't you try to soft-soap
me. I know what's going on, and I'm not sure I ap-
prove."

His father winked at him and grinned. "Now look,

Mother," he told Mrs. Davis, "you know you're just as tickled as I am. When a boy his age is picked to drive in the Granite State, it's a mighty big honor. Win or lose, son, we'll be pulling for you."

The boy's shoulders squared. Suddenly his nervousness was gone and he felt wonderful.

"You'd better get up in the stands if you want good seats," he told his parents. "They'll be starting to fill up soon."

Hartley Martin and his wife were standing by. "You go ahead with the Davises, Polly," said Mr. Martin, "and I'll join you in a few minutes."

When they had gone, he came over to Shad.

"I've got something here for you," he said, taking a folded piece of paper from his wallet. "I'll keep it for you till after the race, but I thought you'd like to see it now."

Shad spread out the paper and nearly fell over backward. It was a check, made out in his name and signed by the Treasurer of the State of New Hampshire. It was for $500!

"That's the reward for Harko Dan," the dairyman told him. "Chief Rooney and I got 'em to put it through a little faster than usual. Now all you've got to worry about is driving Cedar's Boy."

Shad handed the check back to him with a grin of delight. "Thanks, Mr. Martin," he said. "Show it to my mother. Maybe it'll make her feel better about the race."

· · ·

The boy's long legs, neatly encased in the moleskins, felt as if they were made of rubber as he walked behind the sulky into the paddock. Yance, acting as groom, led the proud red pacer. The word had spread among the horsemen that a high school kid was going to drive Martin's big three-year-old, and all their eyes were on him. Some were speculative, some openly hostile, a few friendly. He could feel a flush mounting to his cheeks, but he returned their glances boldly.

There were eight other horses in the enclosure. Outside the fence, hundreds of people jostled each other, trying to get a glimpse of their favorites.

"Hi, Shad!" yelled a boyish voice, and he looked up quickly. 'Poleon, Hank and Bud were standing there together. He waved to them and some of the other drivers laughed.

The band music died down and an order crackled over the loud-speaker. "Calling race number three— the Granite State Stake—open to trotters and pacers with records of two-twelve or better. Best out of three heats, for a purse of five thousand dollars to the winner!"

There was a moment's silence, then—"Drivers up! Parade your horses, one at a time, past the judges'

stand. Take your starting positions in the paddock
and come out as you're called."

Cedar's Boy had drawn fifth position in the field of
nine and there was a figure 5 on the oval plate that
jutted skyward from the crown strap of his bridle.
Yance guided him into line and Shad mounted the
sulky.

Chansonette, with Jake Jarvis up, had the pole and
was called out first. Next came Jester, driven by Luke
Benton. The third horse was an angular brown trotter
named Go-Devil, and the fourth was Mischief Direct,
with Ken Wicks holding the lines.

Yance fastened the bay pacer's checkrein and looked
encouragingly at Shad. There was a roaring in the
boy's ears. Then he heard the words—"Number five—
Cedar's Boy. Owner, Hartley Martin. Driver—" there
was a moment's hesitation, and Shad's cheeks burned
as he turned the horse to pass the stand. At last the
voice went on—"Driver, Melvin Davis."

He closed his ears to the ripple of laughter that ran
through the crowd, and concentrated on following
Billy Randall's instructions. Once past the end of the
stand he let Cedar's Boy out in a warm-up jog as the
drivers ahead of him were doing. They went at a fair
clip clockwise around the upper curve, then slowed
their horses and waited for the rest of the field to catch
up. Turning, they jogged back the way they had come
till they reached the head of the stretch.

As the old trainer had predicted, Shad felt cool now. The first row was lining up in pretty good order and he took Cedar's Boy to the outside, looking across to make sure he wasn't ahead of the man on the pole. The four horses in positions six to nine were in the second line as they started down the track.

The speed picked up. Out of the side of his goggles Shad could see the even line of horses and it looked like a fair start. But at the last moment Go-Devil charged out in front and the bell clanged angrily.

"Mr. White," barked the starter, "get that trotter under control. If you can't hold him you'll be disqualified. All you'll get is one more chance."

The score hadn't hurt the horses. They were more businesslike as they turned again at the head of the straightaway, but Jarvis made some scathing remarks.

"Looks like we've got *two* boy wonders drivin' in this race," he sneered. "When'd you get out o' diapers, White?"

They came down again, a little faster than before, Shad thought. The other drivers held back at the line and Chansonette spurted ahead.

"Go!" yelled the starter and Shad's heart gave a leap. This was it!

There was a real temptation to let the pacer go all out in the battle around the first turn, but he remembered Billy Randall's coaching. Instead of trying to pass the leaders on the curve, he edged in toward the middle of the track, content to be going sixth or seventh. They stayed well bunched up the backstretch, but Shad figured the pace was fast enough to tire some of the weaker horses. He'd get a chance to move up when that happened.

It came sooner than he expected. Rounding the upper turn, Go-Devil dropped back, and so did two others. Shad lifted the reins and the red pacer's ears pricked up as he quickened his easy stride. Coming down the stretch he was in fourth place. The blue roan mare still held the pole, with Jester pacing powerfully right on her flank. Outside, and only half a length back, was Mischief Direct.

Shad brought Cedar's Boy up gradually till he was right behind Benton's sulky. He might have gone wide and tried to pass Wicks on the backstretch, but that would have taken something out of his horse. His orders were to save the big pacer in the first heat.

There was a three-horse race in front of him as they hit the final straightaway. Wicks was making his bid with Mischief Direct, and the roan mare answered with a terrific burst of speed under Jarvis' whip. Jester faltered and Shad pulled Cedar's Boy to the left, cutting through on the rail behind Chansonette. He crossed the finish line in third place, a nose ahead of Benton's black stallion, while the crowd roared its excitement.

Yance met them at the gate, ready to loosen the

checkrein and lead the big bay to the stable. Shad jumped down and walked beside him.

"Sorry we didn't take the heat," he said. "There wasn't much chance to break through."

"You drove it right," answered the gypsy. "Just the way we planned it. You sit down an' get a rest while I walk him. Ol' Billy's taking a squint at the others, but he'll be back pretty quick."

In a few minutes the boy saw Randall limping rapidly toward them. His blue eyes were bright and he was rubbing his gnarled old hands with satisfaction.

"Nice heat, son," he told Shad. "Way I figger it, Chansonette an' Jester pretty well killed 'emselves off. You heard the time? Two-seven-an'-a-half. An' that last lap was a dinger. The hoss to watch, this next heat, is the gray—Dusty Peter. Mel Grant's drivin' him an' he took it easy like you did. But he was right up there in fifth place at the finish. Mischief Direct has plenty left, too. One of 'em's likely to set the pace, an' you stay with 'em. Give Cedar's Boy room to move an' he'll come through."

The fifteen-minute rest period was over. There was no parade this time. At the call Shad mounted and drove out on the track.

There was some confusion at the head of the stretch as the drivers wheeled into their newly assigned positions. Jarvis turned Chansonette a foot or two from Shad's sulky and the boy ducked when the mare bared her teeth at him. There was meanness in every line of her snakelike head and in her wicked, rolling eyes. But in that slim slate-blue body there was speed, as well.

By virtue of her close win in the first heat she still had the pole. Next to her was Mischief Direct, and Cedar's Boy now had the middle position in the front line, with Jester and the lanky gray beyond him.

They came down raggedly for a score. The pole mare was obviously loafing and the starter told her driver so. Jarvis was nettled. On the second try, he had her really trotting. The other drivers picked up the pace and they whirled down to the line in the fastest start Shad had ever seen. There was no recall bell. They were off, flying.

Ken Wicks must have been expecting Jarvis to pull that trick, for his brown mare was at top speed when they crossed the line, and in the next hundred yards she darted ahead to steal the pole. Cedar's Boy had caught the contagion, too. Shad didn't have to urge him to keep up. Going into the turn he was a stride ahead of Chansonette on the outside, his head just lapping Wicks' wheel.

Shad kept him there, following orders. On the backstretch, where the noise of the crowd was fainter, he could hear Jarvis swearing at him.

"Don't try to box me, you punk!" the driver yelled. "Look out—I'm comin' through!"

The boy felt a chill down his back, but he didn't

flinch. He thought Jarvis was bluffing, and as the seconds passed he knew he was right.

They rounded the curve into the straightaway and Shad caught sight of the gray, coming down fast on the outside. The big trotter had tremendous reach and he was using it now as he made his bid for the lead. He passed Cedar's Boy, passed the pacing mare and cut for the pole on the lower turn.

Shad lifted the reins and called his horse by name. Cedar's Boy settled lower to the ground and his red haunches pumped faster. Joyfully he took out after the new leader. Shad let him close the gap till he was pacing just behind Grant's sulky. The backstretch was gone now, and the other horses were lengths to the rear. All the way around the curve the boy wondered how long Dusty Peter could keep it up. He knew Cedar's Boy was pacing with just about all he had, but still the gray trotter gave no sign of slowing.

As they entered the last stretch they were met by a solid wave of sound. Shad couldn't hear his own voice urging the pacer on, but the horse knew why he was being taken wider, with open track ahead. He put back his ears and the fury of his going almost lifted the boy out of the seat.

Shad bent low to cut down wind resistance. He saw Grant use the whip on the gray and an exultant laugh came into his throat. What good was a whip when you were driving Cedar's Boy? This was where heart counted—the will to win. And the red three-year-old had it.

Mel Grant was back of him now, out of sight, and Shad was looking at Dusty Peter's rump—then his withers—finally his head, close alongside. And they were under the wire!

NINETEEN

IT took the rest of the straightaway and half the lower curve to get the red pacer eased down so that he could be turned.

Jogging him back, Shad's joy in victory was clouded by uncertainty. He had never driven a horse in an all-out effort before, and he wondered if he had taken too much out of the gallant three-year-old. Cedar's Boy was still breathing hard and his heaving sides were dark with sweat. But his ears were up and his action seemed smooth enough.

As they passed the stand the cheering crowd suddenly quieted to catch the announcement over the loud-speaker.

"Winner of the second heat, Number Five—Cedar's Boy. Second, Number Seven—Dusty Peter. Third, Number Four—Mischief Direct. Time—" the voice paused for greater effect—"Time, two minutes, four seconds flat—a new record for this track!"

Yance and Billy Randall ran out on the track to meet them. The gypsy's dark face was tense but his eyes were alight with pride as he took the horse's head.

"Two-four!" Randall panted. "Why, that's durn near old Cedar's record—good as he ever paced on a half-mile track! We got a hoss here, Yance."

"Sure have!" the gypsy agreed. "An' we got a driver, too. If I wasn't afraid o' turnin' Shad's head, I'd say he did pretty good in that heat."

"What about Cedar's Boy?" Shad asked. "Do you think he's got enough left?"

"Tell you better when I see how he looks ten minutes from now," Yance replied. "But offhand I'd say he's as fresh as any of 'em. We'll find out what Billy thinks when he comes back from the paddock."

The blanketed horse's head was down, as Yance walked him back and forth, but he was breathing easily again. The trainer took the blanket off and rubbed his sweaty hide with sacking.

"He's tired," Yance said at length. "But he'll do another mile as fast as he has to. I can tell by the look in his eye."

Randall returned a moment later. There was a shade of uneasiness in his crinkly smile, and he looked the pacer over with care before he spoke.

"Jake Jarvis is up to somethin'," he said, at last. "I don't trust him further'n I could throw an anvil. He saved the mare that last heat—come in most a furlong

back—an' she looks mighty pert right now. Keep yer
eye on Jarvis, Shad. He's yeller, but he's tricky, an' he
wants this race bad."

The boy tried to hide the shaking of his hands as
he pulled on the driving gloves. That last heat had
taken something out of him, too.

"I don't want the whip," he told Yance. "It just gets
in my way."

The trainer nodded. "Reckon you don't need it,"
he said. "The colt won't quit. No telling who'll try to
get the lead this time. You'll just have to drive your
own race."

He gave the boy a smile of encouragement and the
sulky went past him through the gate.

There was no spirited prancing as the horses went
up the track. The overeagerness had been wrung out
of them, and the drivers, too, were gruff and silent. All
except Jarvis.

"Well, well," he jeered. "Look who's on the pole!
Better enjoy it while you can, punk—you won't keep
it long!"

The words were just the tonic Shad needed. They
roused his fighting blood and stiffened his backbone.
Flushing a little, he swung Cedar's Boy into position
beside the rail. The others were turning and settling
into their places. He glanced along the front line to
make sure they were ready and the bay horse began to
gather speed.

Whatever Jarvis' plan was, it didn't involve breaking ahead at the wire. They made a surprisingly even
start and the starter screamed "Go!" almost in Shad's
ear.

Gradually the boy lifted the pace, watching out of
the side of his goggles for the expected challenge. He
could hear the pounding of many hoofs close behind
as they rounded the lower turn, but no one tried to
pass. They were letting him set the pace.

Shad wasn't sure he liked it, and Cedar's Boy, too,
seemed uncertain. He kept cocking an ear back as if
he wondered what was happening.

"All right," called his young driver encouragingly.
"Don't wait for 'em, boy. Just keep going nice an'
smooth."

He knew the first lap would be slow, but that wasn't
what bothered him. It was the tense waiting for Wicks
or Grant or Jarvis to make his move.

The crowd wanted more action and yelled for it as
the field swept past, down the straightaway. Now it
would come, thought Shad, and took a firmer grip on
the reins. And sure enough, the rhythm of hoofbeats
quickened. Close alongside, a horse's head came by.
It was the big black stallion, pacing powerfully, his
crimson nostrils flaring.

Shad had forgotten Jester since the first heat, but the
black horse showed no sign of weakness now. He was

past Cedar's Boy and cutting in for the rail before the
young pacer could open up. Now, as Shad got his
horse going fast enough to overhaul the black, another
trotter began to inch past. The boy found himself
neatly boxed, and to make his humiliation more complete he saw it was the roan mare that had come up to
bar his way.

Jarvis snarled something at him and leered vin-
dictively. All Shad could do was swallow his anger and
try to plan a way out. They were well around the
turn and entering the backstretch now. He braced his
feet and pulled, checking the red pacer, easing him
back. At last he had room to swing to the right, behind Chansonette, and there he had to stay while still
another horse passed him. This time it was Mischief
Direct. Ken Wicks shot him a friendly grin but the
veteran had his own race to drive.

Shad felt a moment's discouragement as he peered
through the dust at the three sulkies blocking his path.
But Cedar's Boy wasn't discouraged. Through the taut
leather of the reins, the boy could feel his eagerness.
He stormed up the track, crowding close on the heels of
the pacing mare. Jester and Chansonette were a length
ahead of Mischief Direct, going neck and neck along
the pole. And now Dusty Peter came charging up on
the inside.

That was how they went around the turn, so closely

bunched, it seemed to Shad a blanket would have covered all five.

They were almost into the straightaway, and he was pulling Cedar's Boy wide for a final try, when he heard a screech of metal and a terrified shout. Ahead, on the left, Jarvis had tried to cut in too sharply in front of the black horse, and Jester had put a foot through his wheel. There was a grinding crash as they hit the fence. The stallion screamed horribly and Shad, pounding past, saw a tangle of smashed sulkies and thrashing legs. For a moment he was so sick he could do nothing but close his eyes and clutch the reins.

But Cedar's Boy knew he was still in a race. When Shad came out of his daze, the big red horse was pacing like a fiend, hauling up on Wicks' mare at every stride. He was magnificent. The boy's heart lifted at the sight and he leaned forward, giving the game pacer all the help he could as they came down to the wire.

.   .   .

Riverdale people still talk about that finish. Old-timers say there was never a heat like it. The time wasn't so fast—two-ten-and-a-half—but the way that kid, Shad Davis, brought the bay colt home by a nose was a real piece of driving. Especially after what happened up the track. "Yes, sir," they say, "the youngster's got what it takes! He'll make a Grand Circuit driver—you wait an' see."

Shad's face reddens when he hears that kind of talk. He knows it was Cedar's Boy who won the race, and he was just lucky to be up behind the best three-year-old in New England.

He remembers driving back past the stand, and how the crowd went wild. He had to hold the red pacer a moment at the gate to let an ambulance come clanging by. Benton and Jarvis were both badly hurt and the big black horse had a broken foreleg. Jarvis, he heard afterward, was barred forever from the tracks.

There was a little circle of people waiting for them at the stable as Yance led the colt back.

Hartley Martin and his wife were there, and Bud, and Uncle John and Aunt Sarah Mason. Hank and 'Poleon stood by old Billy Randall, an awe-struck look on their faces. But it was to his father and mother that Shad went when he climbed down stiffly from the sulky.

Mrs. Davis put her arms around him. "I'm—I'm mighty proud of you, Melvin," she said. There was an odd choke in her voice and Shad saw that her cheeks were wet.

"Aw, gee, Ma," he begged. "Don't cry. I promise I won't do it again."

She smiled at him. "Oh, yes, you will," she said firmly. "I guess you're cut out to be a driver an' I won't stand in your way."

Hartley Martin chuckled and patted him on the back.

"That's right," he told the boy. "Soon as you're through school, Yance and I want you on the payroll. By that time we'll have a pretty good string to put on the Fair Circuit—or maybe the Grand. Cedar's Boy and Redwood and Sequoia ought to be in top shape, and the Polly Flinders filly and little Caribou'll be coming along. What do you say?"

Shad felt his knees trembling. He groped for the feedbox and sat down.

"Gosh!" was all he could answer.

"You don't have to decide yet," the dairyman told him. "Maybe you've got some other career in mind. But born horsemen aren't easy to find, and we think you're one. A trainer and driver with the real touch can make a good living at it all his days. I'll give you a hundred a month to start."

Shad didn't answer for a minute. He got up and went over to Cedar's Boy. Yance had the harness off now and was rubbing the pacer down. The boy put an arm around the horse's drooping head and stroked his nose. Velvet lips nuzzled at his fingers.

"Mr. Martin," he said, "that's a mighty generous offer, an' I'll take it. But it isn't the money. I guess I'd work for nothing if I could be around a horse like this. I'll see you soon as school's out next spring."

Old Billy Randall tossed his hat in the air.

"Attaboy!" he yelled. "Bud Martin, you're a lucky feller. You got a stable full o' Cedar's young 'uns—you got Yance—an' now you got Shad Davis. Durned if I know what more a harness hoss man could ask!"